FC FARCE

DARRYL BARKWILL

Copyright © 2025 Darryl Barkwill

All rights reserved.

No part of this book may be reproduced, stored in a retrieval system, or transmitted in any form or by any means without the prior written permission of the author, except in the case of brief quotations for review purposes.

This is a work of fiction. Any resemblance to actual events, teams, or persons — living or dead — is purely coincidental.

Not even VAR can overturn these rights.

ISBN 9798308318729

Independently published

Book cover by Ashley Crossland

Contact me on instagram: @darrylbarkwill

CHAPTER 1

BIRTH OF FC FARCE

'It's quite simple,' the stern-faced council representative explained at a hastily arranged meeting. 'You either repurchase the ground from us, or we'll put the club into administration. The upkeep costs are unsustainable, and we're done footing the bill.'

Henlon Wanderers' owners exchanged nervous glances, knowing full well they didn't have the funds. Outside, a murmur of protest echoed from the streets where loyal fans gathered, their banners pleading for a solution. But inside, it felt like the end was already written. Henlon Wanderers were teetering on the brink of collapse. The council's stance meant that if the ground wasn't sold in a matter of weeks, it was inevitable that the club would fold.

Trevor Farce, a flamboyant local and lifelong fan, watched the situation unravel with a sinking heart. Fond childhood memories flashed through his mind — his father holding him aloft on the terraces, watching wide-eyed as 11 dark green-kitted heroes battled to overcome their opponents.

Of course, that was only part of the fun. He'd watch with amusement as his dad let his emotions get the better of him, bemoaning every decision that the referee dared give the other way. One time, his father completely saw red, launching his favourite meat pie at the referee.

Trevor Farce's audacious personality had enabled him to thrive in life. A stocky, larger-than-life character, he'd stumbled through various failed jobs and ventures before finding his true calling in the most unlikely place, behind the counter of a butcher's shop. He took to it like he'd been born with a cleaver in his hand.

'You'll go far in this game, lad,' his boss once said with a wink, as young Trevor sliced through a cut with expert precision. A few years later, he opened his own premises. 'Trevor's Tenderloins' soon became the most prominent butcher's in the region.

In honour of his dad's memorable misdemeanour, he also began selling hot pies, supplying his beloved Henlon Wanderers and other football clubs throughout the North West. In time, he was living a very comfortable lifestyle and had cash to burn. On one occasion, that's precisely what he did, accidentally setting fire to a wad of notes stashed in his pastry oven.

With Henlon Wanderers' situation worsening by the day, Trevor sat in the back of his butcher's, staring blankly at the day's receipts. His mind wasn't on cuts of beef or pork chops. It was on his beloved football club. Life had been good to him — but he couldn't imagine it without Henlon Wanderers.

Lying awake that night, heart pounding and eyes fixed on the ceiling, Trevor realised he couldn't just sit back and do nothing.

I'll do it, he vowed, before drifting off to sleep feeling 10 times lighter.

The next day, he took a deep breath and entered the vast council office. The stuffy receptionist barely let him through the door.

'You're here about buying a football club?' she said, frowning. 'Ugh, let me see if anyone's available.'

Trevor tapped his foot impatiently as he was passed off between various staff members, each more dismissive than the last. Finally, he was ushered into a meeting room, where he slapped his business plan on the table and launched into a confident pitch — outlining his vision to purchase the ground and take over Henlon Wanderers. The council representatives exchanged uneasy glances, realising with horror that this crackpot butcher might need to be taken seriously.

The council leader was a man named Peter Oddsworth. Or 'Peter Jobsworth' as Trevor sarcastically christened him, after negotiations hit one stumbling block after another. Secretly, the council really liked the idea of the club disappearing. Even if they sold the ground to Trevor, they would still have to deal with transport logistics, policing, and issuing countless matchday safety certificates. In the council's eyes, letting Henlon Wanderers die peacefully would make life so much easier.

After numerous missed phone calls and excuses, Peter Oddsworth begrudgingly agreed to a follow-up meeting. 'I can see you've put a lot of thought into your plans,' the sharply dressed council leader told Trevor, without a hint of sincerity. 'But have you considered section 69.14 of the Transport Act? I'm afraid your proposal fails to address this...'

Trevor threw up his arms. 'This is pointless,' he growled, barely able to keep his voice steady. Oddsworth's smug expression didn't falter.

'You've made your stance crystal clear, but trust me — this is far from over.' He stormed out, the door rattling in its frame behind him.

Undeterred, Trevor took his campaign to the local paper. 'Mr Oddsworth is a busybody fool, blocking my plans for no good reason,' he fumed as the reporter scribbled down every word. 'I urge everyone in Henlon to get behind my campaign.'

His rallying cry had the desired effect. 'Oddsworth's ruining this town!' roared locals at a packed pub, slamming their pints on the table.

Outside the council offices, a group of die-hard supporters gathered, furiously waving banners and chanting, 'Save our club!' The anger was red-hot, fuelled by disbelief that the man supposed to be acting in the town's best interests was behaving so bizarrely. Stung by the uproar, Peter Oddsworth made a public statement via the radio.

'Closing down Henlon Wanderers isn't a decision we take lightly,' he concluded unconvincingly. 'But the truth is, it's probably for the best...'

Oddsworth's closing words lit up the town like a furnace. Furious fans flooded the station with calls, their outrage pouring out in a barrage of insults. If the situation hadn't been so serious, it would've made for fantastic radio. After being called every name under the sun by irate supporters, Oddsworth's cool demeanour deserted him. The council leader made a snap decision.

'Fine!' the flustered council leader yelled live on the radio. 'We'll take it to tribunal! Let them decide!'

The tribunal was set for the following week, and when the day finally arrived, the atmosphere was thick with tension. Every seat in the room was taken, with Trevor feeling the weight of the entire town. A loss to the council wouldn't just mean defeat — it would spell the end of Henlon's beloved football club.

A hushed silence fell as the lead judge entered. Trevor composed himself and presented his case with conviction, highlighting the many benefits a football club brings to the community. In response, Peter Oddsworth, immaculately dressed in his trademark blue suit, was relentless in his bid to force the club's closure. Determined to uphold his reputation as a force to be reckoned with, the council leader seemed intent on blocking Trevor's plans at any cost. He'd even prepared a ludicrous presentation outlining his vision for Henlon without its football club.

As the council leader put forward his bizarre counter-plans, the locals started to grow restless, with Trevor fast losing his patience. Finally snapping, the room watched in tense anticipation as he stood up, pointing an accusing finger straight at Oddsworth.

'You, sir, are the biggest prat I've ever heard!' Trevor bellowed, his deep voice shaking the room. The gathered fans erupted into raucous applause, with psyched-up supporters smacking their seats in delight.

The outburst proved to be a key turning point. With the council finally running out of excuses to block the plans, and chants of 'Oddsworth is a wanker' ringing in their ears, the tribunal room fell silent as the lead judge rose to deliver the official verdict.

'We've reached a decision,' he began, his voice echoing in the tense air. Trevor gripped the armrest of his chair tightly. The judge leaned forward, and the packed room collectively held its breath.

'Trevor Farce will be permitted to purchase the stadium on a 20-year loan, payable to the council.'

The audience erupted. Trevor's fist shot into the air, his heart pounding with joy. He'd done it — he'd saved Henlon Wanderers.

The football club was his!

The tribunal couldn't have gone better, with the long-term loan arrangement immediately freeing up funds to buy new players. In the corner, Peter Oddsworth sank in his seat, the colour drained from his cheeks. The decision amounted to a public humiliation.

They'll pay for this, he vowed, his eyes narrowing with fury.

⚽⚽⚽

Buoyed by the verdict, the town brimmed with excitement as the new season approached. Trevor Farce was well-connected in the area, and his contacts proved invaluable. He hired one of the North West's most highly regarded managers at the time, Fred Cotton, who dropped down a couple of divisions to join this exciting proposition.

The team were competing in the lowly Combinations Division One, far down in the football pyramid. The previous season they'd only just survived relegation, but things were very different now. Henlon Wanderers suddenly had a sizeable budget compared to their opponents, with the chairman pouring his wealth into the venture.

With a new manager and several new players in situ, the Trevor Farce era began. Tickets for the season opener at home to Pluckton United were like gold dust and sold out in minutes. On the day of the match, the whole town of Henlon was buzzing. Parents lifted their children onto their shoulders, the carnival atmosphere in full flow as fans flocked to the stadium.

In honour of the new chairman's profession, a mascot dressed as a large sausage came out ahead of kick-off to parade the fans. It backfired when the away supporters pelted hotdogs in the mascot's direction, resulting in the oversized sausage being ushered back down the tunnel. Trevor found the whole thing greatly amusing, reminding him of his dad's infamous pie incident. Nevertheless, the original mascot was restored at the next match.

After that minor hiccup, the real action got underway and could hardly have gone any better. They thumped Pluckton

United 5-1, with the expensively assembled squad butchering the shell-shocked opposition.

At full-time, Trevor charged onto the pitch and grabbed Fred by the shoulders, planting a kiss square on his lips. The fans roared with laughter as Fred wiped his mouth, chuckling and shaking his head in disbelief.

'You're a nutter, Trevor,' he grinned, patting his chairman on the back.

The afternoon's game felt like the start of something special. And sure enough, the good times kept on coming. The rest of the season turned out to be plain sailing, with no further oversized sausage incidents to speak of, and the team won the league with ease.

Amidst the wild celebrations and champagne-guzzling, the chairman allowed himself a few moments of reflection. In just one short year, he'd gone from running a successful local butcher's to the proud owner of his hometown football club. And that same football club were now the champions.

Trevor chuckled to himself. *Are you watching Peter Oddsworth?*

Going into the next season, there was optimism of a second consecutive promotion. They were now competing in the Combinations Championship, and while the opposition would be stronger than the previous year, the team still had ample resources to compete.

Initially, they carried on where they'd left off, gaining 10 points out of a possible 15 and briefly sitting top of the league. But in the end, they weren't able to hit the heights they'd previously reached. The team finished the season in mid-table, which served as a reality check for the chairman after last season's success. And shortly after the final game, manager Fred Cotton disappeared back to his old job in the higher division.

As the years passed, Trevor watched from the stands as his beloved team stumbled through season after season. Each transfer window he spent heavily, but Henlon Wanderers never managed to properly kick on as a football club.

Not exactly what I had in mind, Trevor thought to himself after yet another mediocre showing. The lofty dreams of taking the club far up the football pyramid slowly faded, with various new managers coming and going. They finished Trevor's third season by narrowly missing out on the playoffs, but after several bottom-half finishes, were eventually relegated to the Combinations Division One — back where they'd started.

Undeterred, Trevor Farce continued to put his money where his mouth was. The team were promoted back to the Combinations Championship at the first time of asking. That's exactly where they stayed for the next seven years, until they finally managed to go one better, gaining promotion to the Combinations Premier League for the first time in the club's history.

For Trevor Farce, the journey had taken its toll. When he became chairman 15 years earlier, he'd had lofty ambitions for the club. If you'd asked him at the time, he would have said that Henlon Wanderers would become one of the best sides in the country, plying their trade far higher than the Combinations Premier League. But despite his considerable wealth, he soon discovered just how challenging it was to build a successful football club, and gradually scaled back his expectations.

In later years, he'd also faced significant health issues. His once lively step had become slower, and the colour in his cheeks had faded. The doctors' advice was always the same — cut back on stress, let go of the club. But the advice fell on deaf ears.

'I'll step down,' Trevor would mutter. 'But only after one more promotion.' Now that he'd achieved that milestone, he should've been able to start thinking about selling up and enjoying his retirement.

But fate, as it often does in football, had a cruel twist in store. Ignoring all medical advice, Trevor chose to go out and celebrate his team's promotion with the players and management. The celebrations soon escalated.

'You alright, chairman?' one player asked, concerned at Trevor's reddening face. 'You look a bit flushed.'

'I'm fine!' Trevor snapped. 'Just enjoying myself.'

The chairman continued to party and celebrate with fans like a madman. The excitement proved to be his undoing, as Trevor Farce keeled over and suffered a fatal heart attack. He died in hospital later that evening.

News of Trevor Farce's passing spread quickly throughout Henlon. By midday, the club gates were lined with flowers, scarves, and heartfelt notes from grieving fans. At the local pubs, supporters shared memories and stories about their colourful former chairman.

'Thank goodness he was able to achieve his goal of promotion before he died,' one supporter reflected at his funeral.

'And people say it's the hope that kills you,' his friend remarked thoughtfully.

⚽⚽⚽

Once the dust had settled, attention turned to the situation at the football club, which was rapidly deteriorating. With Trevor's assets frozen, Henlon Wanderers were temporarily unable to meet their day-to-day payments. In theory, the situation would be resolved as soon as the former chairman's estate was passed to his only son, Graham — who would naturally inherit the football club.

Sitting alone in his father's cramped office, Graham Farce felt the walls slowly closing in on him. The dubious honour of inheriting Henlon Wanderers weighed heavier than the stack of unread letters littered across the desk.

Graham didn't live and breathe football like his father. He went to the occasional match and liked to see the team win, but didn't feel the same burning passion. His slight frame and reserved personality were a far cry from the bold and brash nature of his dad.

Trevor's son found himself caught between a rock and a hard place. Risking the club's future would mean incurring the wrath of the whole town and tarnishing his father's proud legacy — a burden Graham was unwilling to carry. Putting his true feelings to one side, he gritted his teeth and braced himself for the road ahead.

But there was a big problem. Among the club's missed payments was the stadium's 20-year loan, which the council had been forced to accept when Trevor Farce acquired the club 15 years ago. With five years still remaining, the missed payment meant the council now had the right to call in the loan and demand immediate repayment of the full balance.

The now ageing council leader Peter Oddsworth, still reeling from being humiliated at the tribunal by Graham's father all those years ago, sensed an opportunity to seek revenge.

'The full balance must now be paid by the 1st of July,' he told Graham, his voice dripping with satisfaction.

'Look, give me a chance here,' Graham pleaded. 'Paying off that loan will cripple the club's finances before I've even started. It's going to be an uphill battle to survive in the Combinations Premier League as it is. Surely you can be more lenient, given the circumstances?'

Oddsworth smirked. 'Rules are rules, Graham,' he purred. 'Nothing personal, of course.'

After checking through the terms of his father's estate, Graham reluctantly phoned Oddsworth back.

'Listen, I've spoken to the trustees; I won't be able to access the estate until the 2nd of July...'

'So?' Oddsworth demanded, relishing Graham's discomfort.

'So... if I really need to pay off this stadium loan, I can do it then. I assume you're okay with that?'

'That's not good enough!' Peter Oddsworth cried theatrically. 'As you know, the deadline is the 1st of July.'

Graham blinked, stunned by what he was hearing. 'You're telling me you won't accept the payment *one day* late?'

'What can I say? Rules are rules,' Oddsworth replied coldly. 'Tell you what — why don't we take it to a tribunal? That'll bring back good memories.'

Graham stiffened. Oddsworth had him completely cornered. 'Well, I suppose we'll have to,' he said resignedly, his voice heavy with defeat.

The atmosphere was as charged as it had been during the tribunal all those years ago. But unlike 15 years earlier, this time luck wasn't on the club's side. With Oddsworth refusing to budge, the lead judge stepped forward before the packed room and delivered his verdict with visible reluctance.

'I have no choice but to rule in the council's favour,' he began solemnly. 'Since the debt cannot be settled until a day later than owed, the club will have to be wound up for 24 hours, before immediately being allowed to reform on the 2nd of July when the debt is cleared.'

Audible gasps echoed around the room. Had they heard him right?

The lead judge pressed on, confirming their worst fears. 'Unfortunately, this means the club can no longer trade under its current name.' He looked visibly shaken as he spoke.

In a surreal twist, the name Henlon Wanderers was no more. As this realisation sank in, the audience exchanged puzzled glances, scratching their heads at the absurdity of it all. Even Graham, staring blankly at the lead judge, struggled to comprehend the shattering news. But there was nothing he or anyone else could do about it.

As the initial bewilderment turned to anger, a smug Peter Oddsworth winked at the fans gathered in the public gallery, relishing his moment of petty triumph. His antics nearly sparked a riot, and security had to bundle him out of the hearing for his own safety. It was, quite frankly, a ridiculous and entirely avoidable scenario. But the decision was final, leaving the club with no choice but to find a new name.

Following the verdict, Graham sat in his new office, staring out at the empty pitch below. How could he rename the club, having only been chairman for five minutes — and a reluctant one at that? He leaned back in his chair and sighed deeply. There was only one group who deserved to choose the club's new name — the fans.

Fed up and bitter, the supporters decided to turn the situation into a joke at the council's expense. In a resounding vote, the club was reborn as FC Farce — an ironic tribute to Trevor and a final two fingers up to Oddsworth.

So after a series of ridiculous events, Henlon Wanderers became FC Farce. But as it would soon turn out, that new name wasn't just a tribute to their late chairman. It was a fitting introduction to the most farcical season imaginable.

CHAPTER 2

PRE-SEASON — A RELUCTANT NEW ERA

'It's different, I'll give you that!' The assembled reporters slapped their knees in hysterics as the newly christened FC Farce's logo was revealed. The fans had meant well when they chose the club's new name, but the hastily designed emblem — resembling a cartoon goat inexplicably kicking its own head — sparked another wave of laughter from the local press.

Graham Farce's painted-on smile wavered as the media sniggered in the background. He forced a chuckle, but the thought circled in his head. *What on earth am I doing here?*

There wasn't too long to dwell on the absurdity of the situation. The laughter still rang in Graham's ears as he stood alone in his office, staring blankly at a calendar marked with the words: Pre-season training. FC Farce's new chairman shuddered.

Since being thrust into his new role, Graham had handled everything thrown at him as best he could. The 2nd of July date had come and gone, allowing him to finally access the estate and settle up all the outstanding payments. Including the now infamous council loan.

It was a strange dynamic for Graham. Of course, he didn't blame his dad. But he couldn't shake the resentment of taking over a club that he didn't even want. Whether he liked it or not, Graham knew he was stuck with it for the time being. No one would be queuing up to buy a recently liquidated team called FC Farce.

Staring out of the window, the chairman shrugged. 'May as well get on with it.'

It wasn't just the name change that would've put off potential buyers. Graham was horrified to learn that because the club had technically folded, contracts for the entire staff had been terminated — everyone from the players, to the coaching team, to the tea lady. The chairman faced the daunting task of having to re-sign his entire workforce. Every single one of them could leave for free if they wanted to.

The big day arrived to welcome the team back for pre-season training. With mounting apprehension, Graham jogged onto the pitch to greet his players. All five of them.

'Morning, lads. I'm Graham, your new chairman. Are we a bit early?'

One of the lads shrugged, his slender frame defying the usual physique of a footballer. 'No, Mr Chairman. I don't think anyone else is coming.'

'Ah. We've got enough for a five-a-side team then,' Graham quipped.

Normally if players hadn't reported for training, it would've been up to the manager to read them the riot act. No such chance here. The manager had buggered off as well.

Puffing out his cheeks, the reluctant chairman set about building everything back up from scratch. First, he tackled the non-playing staff.

That was fairly straightforward, he thought to himself as yet another staff member signed their new contract. *But what about the players?*

Later that morning, Graham slammed the phone down and crossed the last name off the list pinned to the board. Virtually all his better players, the ones that had helped the team to promotion, had already signed on with other clubs. Not to mention the entire coaching staff who were amongst the very first out the door.

In fact, the only players who agreed to sign new contracts were the five who'd turned up for pre-season training that day. As Graham glanced out the window and watched their disjointed training session, he knew there was a simple reason for that. They all came from the reserves and nobody else wanted them!

With more than a twinge of reluctance, Graham dusted off his father's old contact book and began searching for new recruits.

Where do I start here? This should be a manager's job. How do I know who's good enough to play in this league?

Naturally, rival clubs were sympathetic to Graham's plight and offered to help him out. For instance, one chairman did him a 'huge favour' by selling him one of their 'highly rated forwards' for a bargain price.

'You won't go wrong with this lad,' the kind chairman assured.

'Great!' Graham beamed. 'I appreciate your help.'

Hanging up the phone, the rival chairman laughed his head off. 'Fantastic,' he exclaimed out loud. 'I was just about to release that useless bugger on a free transfer!'

It was a baptism of fire for Graham and he desperately needed some genuine help. He'd only managed to sign a few new players, and frankly, he didn't know if any of them were any good.

A few days later, as Graham was studying a list of potential transfer targets, he received a phone call out of the blue. A mysterious voice greeted him.

'Sorry, who's this?'

'It's Fred, Fred Cotton,' the man replied. 'You may not remember me, but I managed the team 15 years ago when your father first took over. I've always regretted the way I left the club.'

Graham listened intently as Fred took a deep breath and continued. 'I saw all that stuff with Peter Oddsworth and the name change. I'm older and wiser now. I'd love the chance to make amends by managing FC Farce.'

The chairman was stunned. Fred had been a hugely successful manager since he left Henlon Wanderers all those years ago.

'Are you serious?'

'Deadly serious,' Fred assured him. 'I've got a backroom team ready to join me as well.'

Graham didn't need long to make his decision. 'If you were in the room I'd snap your arm off,' he said with a laugh. 'When can you start?'

With the deal done, Graham breathed a sigh of relief. *Finally, a bit of positive news*, he thought.

⚽⚽⚽

The next day, Fred Cotton arrived at the training ground in good spirits. His thinning hair and battered trainers hinted at years of touchline battles; he was not the young man he once was. He knew he was stepping into a difficult situation, but believed his experience alone would be enough to keep the club up.

But the scale of the task soon hit home. The new manager watched in disbelief as his small group of players stumbled over their own feet, fumbling even the simplest of passes. His horror deepened with every botched routine, realising just how bad things were.

'Where's the keeper?' Fred enquired.

'We don't have one,' one of the players replied matter-of-factly.

Fred's smile well and truly vanished. In fact, for the first few training sessions, he was forced to put the ageing kit man in goal. Initially the manager feared for the old man's safety being faced with hard strikes of the ball, but needn't have worried with the players' efforts disappearing hopelessly off target. Frustrated at the lack of progress, Fred went to speak to his chairman.

'Blimey, I didn't know it was quite that bad!' he exclaimed. 'Who are we playing in pre-season?'

The chairman shifted uncomfortably. 'Nobody yet,' he said. Fred's exasperation didn't go unnoticed.

'Look, I know it's not the best situation,' Graham admitted. 'But there's no turning back now. You did just sign a contract to become our manager...'

'Maybe I'll have a word with your mate at the council and see if he can get me out of it,' Fred replied half-jokingly.

Despite the tough circumstances, Fred slowly saw some progress. He called in a few favours and managed to arrange a single pre-season friendly, not ideal but better than nothing. The manager also used his own contact list to sign a few new players.

But bringing in players of sufficient quality was proving

challenging. With the lack of transfer budget, Fred was forced to pursue his third or fourth choice targets, meaning new additions came with their fair share of weaknesses. He quickly realised how difficult it must have been for the chairman, who'd been pretty much guessing.

Most pressingly, with just a couple of weeks until the start of the season, FC Farce still didn't have a keeper. Fred experienced nightmares at the thought of starting life in the Combinations Premier League with a 60-year-old kit man in goal. After more unsuccessful attempts at potential signings, he knocked on Graham's door with an idea.

'Chairman, we desperately need some new players,' Fred explained. 'How about holding an open day for unattached players to come and try out for us? There must be a goalie out there somewhere, and hopefully we can pick up some better players in other positions, too. As it stands, we've only got thirteen lads.'

'I hear you, Fred,' Graham replied, nodding. 'Let's do it.'

People often say that you've got to be a bit mad to be a keeper. And that was certainly a fair assessment of the characters that turned up for the open day. Wincing, Fred and his coaching staff witnessed a mishmash of pretty much everything. Those that were too old, too small, too crazy, or simply too hopeless.

Fred turned to his first team coach Steve and sighed. 'That lad with the grey cap is probably the best keeper I've seen so far.'

'Yeah,' Steve agreed. 'And he's only got one arm.'

Fred was on the verge of giving up. Eventually, he spotted a young hopeful named Rupert Smith. You could hardly miss him, with his rotund figure easily filling the goalposts. He went by the nickname of 'Smithy', after the character from *Gavin and Stacey*.

'What do you think?' Fred asked Steve.

'Hmm,' he pondered, stroking his chin. 'He's got a good kick on him and looks a half-decent shot stopper, but useless coming off his line. I haven't seen anyone better, though.'

Through gritted teeth, Fred Cotton signed Smithy and another five-foot goalie nicknamed 'Shorty' as backup. Other players eventually showed glimpses of promise, but not without their flaws, much like the existing players in the squad. Fred took a deep breath and snapped up a few of these rough diamonds. Now up to eighteen players, the new manager finally had something resembling a squad as FC Farce approached their one and only pre-season friendly.

The friendly was a home fixture against Bashton United, plying their trade two divisions lower than FC Farce. Watching his eager-to-impress players warm up, new manager Fred Cotton felt strangely confident about the game at hand. Despite his reservations about the cobbled-together squad, training had gradually improved, and he felt the team were starting to gel. He was learning about the strengths and weaknesses of his players, and while there were undoubtedly more weaknesses than strengths, Fred was determined to get the best out of them.

Facing a lower league team at home felt like an opportunity to score a few goals and build some confidence. Fred did have deeper concerns about some of his players, particularly Smithy, who seemed to be constantly out of breath even though he hardly moved. But overall the manager was looking forward to seeing the new-look team in action. Meanwhile, Graham Farce watched on with a degree of trepidation. He had no idea what to expect as FC Farce prepared for his first game as chairman.

After Smithy signed for the club, the ageing kit man was able to go back to his normal day job. Old Bill, as he was affectionately known, had been at the club for many years. He was very much part of the furniture, although no one quite knew how he'd gotten the job in the first place. Now that he was no longer the temporary keeper, Old Bill's sole responsibility was ordering the kit and laying it down in the dressing room. The trouble was, in his old age he was getting rather forgetful, not to mention hard of hearing.

Watching his players warm up in their training gear, Fred wondered why no one was wearing the new kit yet.

'Bill, where's the kit for today?'

'Huh?' Bill replied blankly.

Fred flinched. 'You did remember to place the order?'

Bill scratched his head and stared blankly into space. After a quick investigation, Fred was horrified to find the full kit was still in the online shopping cart. He nearly blew his fuse, but there was no time for an inquest. The match was due to start in an hour, and the team didn't even have a kit. The manager took a sharp intake of breath and went to speak to the referee.

'There's been a mix-up,' Fred said grimly. 'Long story short — we don't have a kit. Can we play in our training gear?'

The ref examined the mismatched group with bemusement. 'I see. Well, the socks and shorts are fine, but those training tops are no good. They're all in different colours — they need to be matching.'

Fred looked to the heavens. Suddenly, there was serious danger of FC Farce's only pre-season game being called off.

From the stands, Graham noticed there seemed to be a bit of a commotion on the pitch, and made his way down to see what was happening. Fred saw his chairman coming and grimaced before jogging over to deliver the verdict.

'Erm, bad news,' Fred began slowly. 'Old Bill forgot to order the kit. The ref's threatening to call off the match.'

'What!' Graham shouted. 'That can't happen. What would the fans say?' Graham motioned towards the ref. 'Let's go and speak to him.'

Reluctant or not, this was his first game as chairman, and he wanted to get off to a positive start. The chairman and manager went to appeal to the referee's better nature.

Eyeing both men wearily, the ref's stance remained. 'There's nothing I can do. It's the league's rules. Either get matching shirts in time for kick-off, or you'll have to forfeit the game.'

An increasingly flustered Graham turned to his manager. 'If this game is abandoned, we'll get a huge fine. We can't throw away more money after paying off that stadium loan. Surely there's *something* we can do?'

Help came from an unlikely source. A young matchday kiosk staff member named Tim trotted over.

'Hi, chaps!' Tim grinned enthusiastically. 'I couldn't help overhearing about the issue with the kits. Along with my job here, I also work part-time at the local college around the corner...'

'So?' Fred snapped.

Tim's enthusiasm didn't wane. 'Well, I could go and get some white T-shirts from lost property. There's bound to be enough there. I've got the key in my pocket.'

Fred didn't sound overly impressed with this suggestion. 'My team can't play in a load of old children's tops!' he cried.

'No, no, no! They're college-age shirts,' Tim said. 'About 17 and 18-year-olds. It'll be fine.'

Looking the young staff member up and down, Graham made a quick decision. 'Look, we don't have any other options. We can't afford to forfeit this match.' The chairman briefly paused, before giving a decisive nod. 'Tim, go and get that kit.'

Fred shook his head in exasperation. By now his pre-match confidence had all but evaporated.

With minutes to spare before kick-off, the shirts were duly delivered.

'Here you go!' eager to impress Tim exclaimed. 'And I've written FC Farce on the front for you!'

The players exchanged sceptical glances as they squeezed into the tight white shirts, etched in black ink that was already fading. Tim had clearly meant well, but the scruffy handwritten labels just made the whole thing look even more ridiculous.

Smithy tugged at his tight kit, grimacing. 'This is a joke, right?' It barely covered his stomach.

'You look great!' Tim exclaimed.

'Does it look OK, boss?' Smithy asked, turning to Fred.

'You look great Smithy,' Fred lied. The fabric was practically bursting at the seams. But at least the team had a kit and could now play the match.

In hindsight, they shouldn't have bothered. Much to Fred's

despair, lowly Bashton United thrashed FC Farce 5-0. To make matters worse, heavy rain caused the black pen from their T-shirts to drip all over the pitch — a rather pathetic sight worthy of the performance. Fred Cotton glared at well-meaning Tim, now cowering in the safety of his kiosk.

Travelling fans treated the glum FC Farce supporters to a rousing rendition of, 'You've got no kit, and you're shit.' At the final whistle, the players couldn't get off the pitch quickly enough. In the stands, Graham sat with his head in his hands. Not ideal preparation with the start of the season just one week away.

The performance hardly endeared the reluctant chairman to his inherited project. He tried to put on a brave face at the result, but it didn't take a genius to realise that the team had major problems. Graham also sensed Fred's frustration at the debacle, and was concerned he'd genuinely want to pack it in already. Brushing his own negative thoughts to one side, Graham phoned Fred to get his take.

Deep down, the friendly disaster had firmly reinforced Fred's initial concerns about the team's ability to compete in the Combinations Premier League. But he put on a show of defiance for his chairman.

'Listen, Graham,' he began, after a brief pause, 'I've seen it all — the highs, the lows... and whatever this is. We'll get through it.'

Graham breathed a sigh of relief. 'Thank goodness for that — thanks, Fred. Oh, and rest assured, Old Bill will only be responsible for preparing the kit from now on, not ordering it.'

⚽⚽⚽

Two days before the start of the season, the chairman and manager were due to attend a 'Meet the fans' forum. Both men were nervous to face supporters after the disastrous friendly result, but saw it as an early opportunity to make amends. The event was set for 6:30pm in The Brown Bull — a local pub in the heart of Henlon.

Bracing themselves, Graham and Fred arrived early and ordered a drink before taking their seats at the front of the room. Five minutes before the event was due to start, there was no sign of any fans. In fact, the chairman and manager were literally the only ones in the pub, apart from an old man tucked in the corner reading his newspaper.

'Are you here for the fans' forum?' Fred eventually asked him.

The man looked up, bewildered. 'What are you talking about?'

Graham and Fred exchanged uneasy glances. Surely the friendly hadn't put everybody off?

'And where are my coaching team?' Fred barked. 'They all swore they'd be here to back us up!'

As the clock ticked closer to the start time, there was still no sign of anybody. It appeared that the fans were staying away in response to last week's poor defeat. The chairman couldn't help wishing he could also turn his back on the club so easily...

Graham shrugged. 'Oh well, may as well order another round...'

After several beers, an intoxicated Fred opened up to his chairman.

'You know what, Graham,' he slurred. 'I'm going to be honest here. I'm having serious doubts about whether I can get this team going...' Fred leaned towards Graham. 'I'm actually feeling a bit out of my depth here.'

An equally tipsy Graham just chuckled at the admission. 'Oh, I'll go one better. I didn't even want to inherit this bloody farce in the first place!'

'So, what the hell are we actually doing here?' Both men roared with drunken laughter. It was a strange conversation for a manager and chairman to be having.

At least they were kind of on the same page. For better or worse, they agreed to stick with it and do their utmost to keep FC Farce in the division.

'Even if the ungrateful fans can't be bothered to turn up tonight!' Graham snorted.

By now they were several drinks in. Graham excused himself to get some air, and after stepping outside, realised he was well gone. As he tried to steady himself, his phone beeped with several missed calls from Steve, the first team coach. Squinting at this phone, Graham realised there had been no reception at the pub. He phoned Steve back.

'Chairman!' Steve shouted. 'We're all here waiting for you. The fans have been here for over an hour now! Where are you and the gaffer?'

Graham frowned. 'What are you talking about?' he replied, stumbling slightly. 'We've been waiting for you!'

As Steve explained, Graham's stomach dropped, realising with horror that he and Fred were in the wrong pub. The event was at The Bull Arms across the high street, which they'd somehow got confused with The Brown Bull.

He stumbled back inside to find Fred slumped on the bar, his head resting in his arms.

'Fred, wake up!' Graham shook his manager's shoulder. 'We're in the wrong pub! The fans are all waiting for us!'

Fred blinked groggily, barely lifting his head. 'Wrong pub?' he mumbled, squinting as he tried to make sense of the revelation.

'Yes! The fans are waiting for us — come on!' Graham half-dragged Fred to his feet, while the old man with the newspaper looked on in bemusement.

The only trouble was that both men were absolutely wasted. As they staggered over to the correct establishment, Fred could barely string a sentence together, let alone answer any questions. Finally bursting through the door, the packed crowd gave them a huge, ironic cheer.

In a drunken daze, the usually reserved Graham took to the stage and launched into a garbled, blathering speech that nobody could quite understand, apologising about 15 separate times for the evening's cock-up.

At the end of the disjointed ramble, he lost his footing and slipped and fell off the stage. The crowd erupted in laughter, thoroughly entertained by the spectacle.

Far from alienating the fans, the sight of their inebriated

chairman falling on his arse won them over. As the night went on and the drinks flowed, there was a real sense of camaraderie, giving everyone a glimpse of what might carry FC Farce through the turbulent season ahead.

The next day, Graham woke up with a pounding headache. Dry-mouthed and hungover, he tried to call his manager, but there was no answer. He assumed Fred would be sleeping off his own hangover, and prayed that it would at least clear up by Saturday for the season's first league game. Luckily, the players had already been given the day off after a week of double training sessions. Graham braced himself as he flicked open the local newspaper.

Sure enough, there it was — 'Fan Forum Farce!' splashed all over the back pages. But the reporting was all good-natured, recognising that the mishap had been well received and lifted spirits ahead of the season. The report even joked that the chairman's 'sozzled performance' was probably the best thing he'd done since taking over.

Breathing a sigh of relief, Graham chuckled as he reflected on his tenure so far.

In just a few short weeks, I've managed to let the fans turn the club into a public punchline, lose half the squad, watch the team play in a bunch of borrowed school shirts, and fall off the stage in front of the fans. So far, so good...

It had certainly been more eventful than the mild-mannered chairman had wanted or expected. Graham couldn't help but wonder what lay ahead, with the real action about to get underway...

CHAPTER 3

AUGUST – JAPANESE REINFORCEMENTS

Fred's alarm buzzed loudly at 7:30am, yanking him from a deep sleep. Squinting at his phone, he groaned and rolled over, head still pounding from Thursday's antics. Friday had been a write-off spent dodging Graham's calls and nursing his hangover. Then, like a bolt from the blue, he sat up straight. It was matchday — the season's opener.

An odd surge of excitement hit him. For reasons he couldn't place — maybe alcohol-induced optimism or pure delusion — he felt good about their chances against Ostley Rovers. The visitors were firm favourites, but Fred hoped that the week of gruelling double training sessions would pay dividends. If FC Farce could pull off any kind of result, last week's friendly debacle would all be forgotten.

Arriving at the ground with a spring in his step, Fred's nerves kicked in when he saw the two sets of players warming up. Across the pitch, Ostley Rovers operated in slick formations, moving the ball around the team with confidence and precision. By comparison, his lads resembled a group of toddlers learning to walk. It was a sobering sight, and much like the previous Saturday, his initial confidence all but vanished.

Back in the dressing room, the manager defiantly put his concerns to one side.

'They don't look much cop this lot,' Fred lied. 'We can definitely win today. In fact, I think you can beat anyone.'

The pre-season friendly disaster had made Fred question his starting 11. He'd have liked to have made changes, but the sheer lack of options made him stick to the same personnel and basic

4-4-2 formation. Here was the full line-up, with descriptions based on the manager's assessment of his players so far:

Goalkeeper: Rupert 'Smithy' Smith
Decent shot-stopper, useless off his line. Or moving with any type of speed whatsoever.

Right back: Ollie Wright
Fast, but frequently leaves the ball behind. If he could just remember to bring it with him...

Centre back: Clive Harrison (captain)
Tough and fearsome, but like the kit man — slightly deaf. Constant miscommunication sees him marking the wrong players or running the wrong way.

Centre back: Tim Jenkins
A former ballet dancer, graceful in movement but often trips over his own feet.

Left back: Barry McGraw
An unpredictable left foot, with the tendency to send long balls wildly into the stands.

Right midfield: Nelly Patterson
Decent dribbler, but can't cross to save his life. No end product.

Centre midfield: Freddie Thompson
Paralysis by analysis. He'll stop mid-game to ponder his next pass while the opposition takes the ball.

Centre midfield: Gavin O'Donnell
Skilful, but his laid-back attitude often results in him forgetting he's even on the pitch.

Left midfield: Matty Reynolds
His shots are powerful, but control is non-existent. His sole effort in the friendly ended up completely out of the stadium.

Striker: Will Watkins
Scored a screamer in training, then injured himself with an acrobatic celebration. Unpredictable at best.

Striker: Percy Plumb
Talented, but far too hesitant. He waits for the 'perfect' shot and often loses the chance completely.

Despite the less-than-encouraging assessments, the players were ready and raring to go in the dressing room ahead of kick-off. Remember, most had either come from the reserves or were cast-offs from other teams. There were limitations in their abilities, but collectively they had a point to prove.

As the players cracked nervous jokes to take the sting out of the occasion, Fred stood up to address the group. 'Lads, just a few last-minute words.' The players fell silent. 'Ollie, don't forget to take the ball with you.'

'Yes, boss.'

'Gavin, no switching off today.'

'Of course, boss.'

'And Will, no more acrobatics!'

'Got it, boss.'

'Great,' Fred paused and looked at each of his players squarely in the eyes. 'Now, are you ready to go?'

'Yes!' they roared back, jumping to their feet as cries of *'C'mon, FC Farce!'* bounced around the walls.

On cue, a loud ringing bell signalled for the players to enter the tunnel. The psyched-up players charged into the narrow corridor alongside Ostley Rovers. Perhaps they were a little too psyched-up. Much to their opponents' amusement, former ballet dancer Tim Jenkins tripped over and brought half of his teammates down with him in a domino effect.

'Is everyone OK?' Tim muttered sheepishly.

'Yes,' his teammate Will Watkins replied with a grin, pulling the others up. 'C'mon, let's do this.' With that, the team finally entered the pitch for FC Farce's first ever match in the Combinations Premier League.

It was a beautiful August day and perfect conditions for football. As the players emerged from the tunnel to the sun-soaked pitch, this time in a shiny dark green new kit, they were greeted by an almighty cheer from the fans. The pre-season game was probably just under half full with little atmosphere to speak of, but today's crowd was packed and bouncing. As the players took their places, the crowd chanted, 'There's only one Trevor Farce' — in honour of the late chairman.

Sat in his father's former wooden seat in the stands, Graham felt a tear trickle down his face. He couldn't help feeling moved by the tribute.

'Before today's match,' the stadium announcer boomed. 'There will be a minute's silence to remember Trevor Farce. It will start and end on the referee's whistle.'

'Peeeeeep!' The whole ground fell deadly silent. The tribute was impeccably observed, but as more seconds ticked by, it seemed to take an awfully long time.

'Surely it's been a minute by now?' one fan whispered, glancing at his watch.

'It must be...' his mate began. 'Wait, what's going on over there?'

In the middle of the pitch, the ref suddenly started darting around, frantically waving his arms. His whistle had jammed. He kept trying to blow it, but no sound came out, leaving him visibly distressed. It was a remarkable sight — a sea of solemn fans struggling to contain their laughter while the ref charged around the pitch like a madman.

After three excruciating minutes, the fourth official found him a spare whistle.

'Peeeeeep!' With his face flushed, the referee exhaled in relief as the crowd erupted, finally marking the start of the match.

From the first minute, opponents Ostley Rovers took control. The pre-game carnival atmosphere quickly dampened as the home fans witnessed their limited team in competitive action. The away side twice went close to taking the lead in the first few minutes, forcing Smithy into a couple of smart saves.

At the other end, right back Ollie Wright showed off his speed early on, but despite the manager's final instructions, the ball was struggling to stick to his feet. Meanwhile, Clive Harrison's partial deafness led to more than one nerve-racking moment at the back. Mishearing a call for a high line, FC Farce's captain inexplicably ended up marking the centre circle, completely out of sync with the rest of the back four.

From the left, Barry McGraw saw an attempted cross soar high and wide, clearing the stands and narrowly missing a dog walker who leapt to safety, dragging her poor terrier out of the way. His sheepish grin did little to ease the growing frustration amongst supporters. Meanwhile, Ostley continued to dominate possession.

Then, completely against the run of play, FC Farce took the lead. A corner kick turned into a comedy of errors, bouncing off legs, elbows, and one unlucky Ostley Rovers defender before somehow plopping into the back of the net.

'Goal!' The crowd erupted in delirious disbelief, the shock lead reigniting the atmosphere in the ground.

Fred puffed out his chest on the sidelines, hoping to give the impression that the lucky goal had all been part of his tactical genius. He barked instructions at his team, urging the players to kick on and look for a second. Even Graham, typically reserved, found himself on his feet clapping, daring to hope for an unlikely victory.

But Ostley Rovers continued to dominate the game. They controlled possession and launched attack after attack, forcing Smithy into a series of awkward saves. Their inevitable equaliser came just before half-time, a well-placed shot from just outside the box that left Smithy with no chance. Now it was the travelling contingent's turn to celebrate wildly.

Shortly afterwards, the referee glanced at his watch and delivered a shrill blow. FC Farce had made it to half-time level pegging.

Despite Fred's encouraging words at the break, the second half was all Ostley, hitting the post twice and missing several glaring opportunities. FC Farce's defence was in disarray, with Clive and Barry often hopelessly out of position. Ollie's attempts to support the attack left gaping holes behind him. It was through sheer luck and Smithy's unlikely heroics that the scores remained level as the fourth official held up his board for three minutes of added time.

Heart pounding, Fred was desperate for the reprieve of the final whistle. *Just blow up, ref.*

When the referee finally blew for full-time, relief swept throughout the ground. The 1-1 draw felt like a minor miracle. FC Farce's players trudged off the pitch, a mix of satisfaction and exhaustion on their faces. The fans warmly applauded the team, recognising the effort that the players had put in despite Ostley's superiority. On the sidelines, Fred wiped the sweat from his forehead. The performance had done little to convince him of his team's capabilities, but at least they'd come away with a point.

As the players filtered back to the changing rooms, the manager and chairman lingered by the dugout. Fred grimaced and gave the chairman his verdict.

'I've really got my work cut out here, Graham. The lack of quality was glaring.' Fred paused, sighing deeply. 'But I'll give it to them, the lads gave everything. They were outclassed but fought for every ball. Fair play to Smithy, he kept us in it today, although you'd have thought he'd just run a marathon the way he was panting and sweating out there.'

The chairman nodded in agreement, his gaze following the manager as he went to join the players in the dressing room. Graham too was proud of the way the lads had dug in. He chuckled as he imagined his late father Trevor looking down on today's game, kicking every ball in anger and disagreeing with the referee.

I actually enjoyed that more than I thought, the new chairman admitted to himself, dedicating the result to his father.

In less nostalgic matters, Graham knew that the team had gotten away with one; any fool could see that. He also knew Fred would probably knock on his door first thing Monday to ask if he could sign some new players, which was impossible given the club's financial situation. But that was a problem for another day, and he went off to the clubhouse for a well-deserved pint.

Sure enough, early Monday morning Fred asked his chairman if he could have a word. He reckoned they needed at least five new additions to have any realistic chance of staying up. Eyeing his manager intently, Graham didn't pull any punches.

'Look, I'd love to give you some more funds,' Graham said, puffing out his cheeks. 'But we literally don't have the money. Having to pay off that council loan and re-sign our whole team has put a huge hole in the club's finances. We've already overspent on the players we've brought in. You're going to have to make do.'

In his younger days, Fred would've probably run a mile. But the bond he'd built with Graham and his own memories of walking out on Trevor kept him grounded.

'I understand, Graham,' he replied with a nod. 'I'll work with what I've got.'

What he had wasn't a lot though, and the manager's worst fears were realised in the next two games. FC Farce were comfortably beaten 2-0 away at Kibley Town, followed by an embarrassing 4-0 home defeat to Stormford United, who'd been promoted alongside them the previous season. The successive defeats left FC Farce joint bottom of the table.

⚽⚽⚽

The morning after the Stormford match, Fred was stirred from his lie-in by a phone call. Studying his mobile screen, he saw it was Steve, his first team coach.

'What could he possibly want now?' Fred mumbled, tempted to let it ring out. But curiosity got the better of him.

'Morning, gaffer!' Steve's voice was oddly chipper. 'I think I've got you a player!'

Fred squinted. 'A player? From where?'

'Japan — Tommy from Japan.'

Fred stared at his phone blankly. 'Tommy from... *Japan?*' He was starting to wish he hadn't taken the call.

'Hear me out a minute, gaffer,' reasoned Steve. 'My cousin's got this guy called Tommy coming over from Japan to stay with him on a work placement. He says Tommy was the best player for his old team back home, and he could definitely do a job for us.'

Fred was slightly bemused, but the proposition piqued his interest. After all, the team were desperate for reinforcements.

'What do you think, boss?'

Fred went silent for a few moments. 'I'm not sure,' he eventually replied, hesitantly. 'I'll need to see him play first.'

Tommy (real name Tanaka Haruki Yoshitsune) was due to fly over on Wednesday. So after careful consideration, Fred decided to invite him to Thursday's training session. If he was any good, he could sign him up ahead of Saturday's game.

Fred explained the situation to his chairman. 'Are you OK with that, Graham?'

'If he's a free agent, go for it. What have we got to lose?'

'Great.' Fred beamed. 'I just hope he's as good as Steve's cousin says he is...'

The following day, training was going smoothly until Fred called for a new drill.

'Set up for a high press!' he shouted. But FC Farce's partially deaf captain Clive Harrison was slightly out of earshot and thought he heard 'take a rest.' So while his teammates geared up for an intense pressing drill, Clive casually strolled to the sideline, oblivious to the activity behind him.

As the players surged forward, Clive suddenly found himself in the wrong place at the wrong time. Over-thinker Freddie Thompson hesitated just as he was about to make a pass, causing a pile-up of players right where Clive was standing. Clive still thought he was supposed to be resting, and was taken completely by surprise as a tangled mess of limbs and bodies crashed into him.

He hit the ground with a thud, a look of pure bewilderment on his face. Fred rushed over, a mix of concern and exasperation. 'Clive, what on earth are you doing?'

Clive, wincing as he sat up, shrugged. 'Thought you said to take a rest, boss...'

Fred rolled his eyes and sent him off to get checked over. Later, the news came back that the defender had swollen ribs and would be out for the weekend's game. This was all Fred needed with the team already so thin on the ground. With a heavy sigh, Fred turned to coach Steve.

'What position is this Japanese lad?' he asked, resignedly.

'Not sure,' Steve admitted. 'But my cousin says he's built like an absolute brick. I'm sure he'd be fine at the back.'

Fred nodded. 'OK, let's just have a look at him tomorrow. Fingers crossed he's good. We definitely need him now.'

Arriving at training the following day, Steve came rushing over to Fred. Alarm bells immediately started ringing.

'Um, boss,' Steve began, shifting uncomfortably. 'There's been a mix-up with Tommy's flight. He won't land here until Friday night now.'

'What?' Fred shouted, barely believing his ears. 'For goodness sake, Steve — he's landing *Friday night*? There's no time to even see him play before Saturday.'

Steve shook his head. 'Well, what should we do, boss?'

Composing himself, Fred took a moment to weigh up the situation. Without Clive, they only had two recognised defenders on the bench, and he didn't rate either of them. Based on what he'd heard from Steve's cousin, he was hoping to bring Tommy straight into the starting line-up. There was no way he could do that without seeing him first. But maybe he could sign Tommy anyway and stick him on the bench?

After much deliberation, Fred went to Graham, laying out the dilemma.

'Look, it's your call,' Graham said, shrugging. 'I feel bad enough that we can't afford anyone else. If you think signing Tommy is the answer, I'm fully behind you.'

It was an unorthodox solution and a huge gamble. Fred took a deep breath.

'Alright,' he said, squaring his shoulders. 'Let's do it.'

With Steve's cousin acting as the middleman, they managed to get Tommy's details and officially register him as an FC Farce player. They initially signed him up on a one-game-only basis, with the option to extend if it was deemed a success. Worst-case scenario, Fred reasoned, he couldn't be any worse than anything they had. With the deal done, he interrupted the training session to speak to his players.

'Lads, I've just signed a guy called Tommy from Japan,' Fred announced cheerily. 'I've never seen or heard of him, but he'll be going straight into the squad for Saturday's game. Anyway, back to your training drills!'

The players exchanged stunned glances. It was hardly a vote of confidence in their abilities.

⚽⚽⚽

Saturday finally arrived, and the team were playing at home to Poldon Borough. Fred anxiously scanned the car park, eventually spotting the arrival of Steve and Tommy. Catching his first glimpse of the mystery Japanese superstar, Fred was very impressed. Tommy was solidly built, looking every inch the imposing defender they needed. Although his English was limited, his stature and physical presence oozed promise.

Eagerly sizing Tommy up, Fred was tempted to start him. But given the language barrier and the fact Tommy had just arrived from the other side of the world, he decided to stick with the original plan. Tommy would start on the bench.

After an uneventful first 45 minutes, the game against Poldon Borough was still goalless as the teams kicked off for the second half. Neither side had particularly threatened, with FC Farce coping well with Clive's absence. Just before the hour mark, ex-ballet dancer Tim Jenkins went down clutching his ankle. With two first choice central defenders out of the game, the team were in a perilous position.

Wincing, Fred looked at his bench. 'Tommy. You're going on.'

Tommy looked at him blankly. Steve hastily translated, and a light dawned on Tommy's face. He jogged onto the pitch and looked around hesitantly, his expression a mix of wonder and confusion.

As the game continued, Tommy stood still, wide-eyed as the action unfolded around him, only occasionally taking a tentative step in either direction.

'C'mon, Tommy!' his teammates urged. 'Look for the ball!'

The encouragement had no effect. After 10 excruciating minutes of watching his 'Japanese superstar' barely move, Fred's patience finally snapped.

'Get stuck in, Tommy!' Fred bellowed from the touchline, his voice dripping with exasperation.

Tommy took the instruction to heart. The next time the ball came near, he charged at the opposition player with the intensity of a runaway steam train, knocking him clean to the ground. The crowd gasped and the referee's whistle shrieked, but Tommy wasn't done. Clutching the ball in his hands, he sprinted the full length of the pitch with terrified Poldon Borough players darting out of his way.

On the sidelines, Fred stared open-mouthed. 'What on earth is that lunatic doing?' he cried at an equally dumbfounded Steve.

Finally reaching the opposition's goal, Tommy booted the ball high over the bar, sending it soaring into the stands. Grinning from ear to ear, he embarked on a solo celebration, pumping his fists and leaping with joy as his teammates and fans watched on in astonishment.

Recovering from his initial shock, the referee marched over and brandished a straight red card. Tommy's triumphant expression faltered as he realised he must have done something wrong. He trotted past his bewildered teammates and took his seat back on the sidelines. Fred shook his head in amazement. Quite simply, he'd never seen anything like it in all his years in football. Meanwhile, the Poldon player he'd clattered into was still on the ground nursing his injuries.

The incredible moment rattled the opposition. Although FC Farce were down to 10 men, their opponents were visually shaken and started backing out of tackles left, right, and centre. Fred suddenly sensed an opportunity.

'Go forward!' he screamed. Realising something might be stirring, the fans collectively roared the team on.

Despite their numerical disadvantage, FC Farce continued to press forward and attack Poldon Borough with menace. The game remained goalless until the dying moments of the game, when the unpredictable Will Watkins found himself in the right place at the right time. A deflected cross fell to his feet, and with ice-cold precision, he slammed the ball into the roof of the net.

1-0! The crowd exploded with joy.

As the final whistle blew, FC Farce's 10 men celebrated a memorable victory. Fred shook his head, a mix of relief and amazement at the chaotic scenes. Behind him, Graham looked on with stunned delight. He couldn't help being swept up in the euphoria of the crazy win. Supporters celebrated wildly, warmly applauding their Japanese hero and chanting his name. Tommy grinned from ear to ear and revelled in the fans' admiration.

It had been utterly bonkers, but somehow the team had pulled off their first win of the season.

The next day, Fred was again woken from his lie-in by a call from Steve.

The coach sounded flustered. 'Um, boss...' he began sheepishly. 'My cousin has just discovered something. Turns out Tommy isn't actually a footballer. He's a rugby player from a remote Japanese village where rugby is the only sport. He's never seen a football in his life.' Steve paused, catching his breath. 'Sorry, boss.'

Not for the first time that weekend, Fred was speechless, his mind trying to process the absurdity. After a long silence, he burst into laughter.

'Alright, no contract extension then.' Fred chuckled. 'But Tommy will always be remembered as a hero around here.'

CHAPTER 4

SEPTEMBER — TWIN-JUSTICE

First thing Monday morning after their unlikely victory, Fred Cotton and Graham Farce were summoned to an urgent meeting with the football league. The room's atmosphere was a stark contrast to the jubilant chaos of Saturday's game. The stern-faced league official fixed them with a steely gaze.

'Mr Cotton, Mr Farce,' he began. 'Can you explain how you came to field a player who didn't know the rules of football?'

Fred and Graham exchanged nervous glances. For Graham, this tense environment brought back memories of the recent name-changing tribunal. He gestured for Fred to speak first.

Fidgeting with his shirt cuff, Fred cleared his throat. 'Tommy came highly recommended,' he began cautiously, glancing sideways at Graham. 'We... well, we didn't dig deep enough into his background.'

'I'd say that's evident, Mr Cotton,' the official interrupted, raising an eyebrow. 'Given he was a rugby player...' The official turned to Graham. 'Mr Farce, I know you haven't been chairman long, but surely you must have known the importance of verifying a player's background?'

Graham nodded. 'Of course. But things have been a bit... hectic since I took over. With the club's name change, re-signing staff, and everything else. It's not an excuse, just the reality of how it's been.'

The official sighed, eyeing Graham and Fred wearily.

'Well,' he began. 'Technically, your club hasn't broken any rules. And since the player your... *enthusiastic* substitute clattered into isn't seriously injured, I'll let you off with a warning.'

Fred and Graham's eyes met with relief, but the official raised a hand — he wasn't finished.

'That said, let me be perfectly clear,' he continued. 'FC Farce have already made more than enough headlines this season. Make sure you keep out of trouble from now on.'

'Of course,' Graham replied, nodding vigorously. 'We're grateful for your understanding.'

The official gave a curt nod, signalling the end of the meeting.

Later that morning, Fred stood at the edge of the training ground with his eyes locked on Will Watkins. The forward sprinted down the pitch, relentless yet clumsy, like a puppy chasing its tail. One minute, he overhit a cross into the bushes. The next, he unleashed a shot so fierce and accurate it nearly burst through the net. Fred's lips tightened.

'Steve, have you got a minute?' Fred shouted towards his first team coach.

Steve's attention turned away from the thick of the training session. He trotted over to see the manager.

'What is it?'

'Steve, I want you to focus your attention on Will Watkins,' Fred instructed. 'There's a player in there somewhere, he just needs to find consistency. But the quality of his winning strike on Saturday shows his potential.'

Steve nodded, a hint of apprehension bubbling inside. Working with Will was always an experience — you never quite knew what you were getting. But he was eager to make up for the cock-up with Tommy. Taking a deep breath, Steve jogged over to his new project.

The coach started with some basic shooting drills. He set up some targets in the goal and handed Will a ball, instructing him to aim for the bottom corner. Will nodded enthusiastically and took a powerful shot. The ball sailed through the air, missing the target by a mile, instead hitting a tactics board and sending bits of paper scattering everywhere. His teammates watching nearby fell about laughing.

Ignoring their lack of encouragement, Steve set up a new target — an old tire hung in the top corner of the goal. 'Hit the tire, Will,' Steve urged. The player took a deep breath and lined up his shot. This time the ball flew over the goal, before hitting a fence and cannoning back, narrowly missing Steve's head. The coach couldn't help but be impressed by Will's raw power, even if it was misdirected.

As the session progressed, Steve noticed glimmers of improvement. When Will connected properly, his shots had both power and accuracy, reminiscent of his winning strike on Saturday. Will's biggest obstacle, Steve thought, was channelling his energy productively. His flashes of brilliance were often undermined by his unpredictability, which had held him back from making it at a higher level.

Pinning all hopes on Will was risky, but the extra training paid off. In September, Will hit a purple patch, scoring four goals in three games. He scored both goals in a narrow 3-2 loss away to Dryden Town, before finding the back of the net again in a 1-1 draw at home to Levelston United. Finally, he scored a consolation in a 4-1 loss away to Reefton United.

'How about that, eh?' Coach Steve said to Fred the following week, revelling in the success of his project.

'Yes, great job. That gets you off the hook for Tommy,' Fred replied with a wink. 'Let's just hope he can keep up his consistency.'

The downside was that FC Farce only had one point to show for his impressive run, sitting fourth from bottom and just outside the relegation zone. Nevertheless, he had proven himself as integral to the team's survival hopes.

FC Farce's last game in September was at home to Worton United. Despite the team's poor run, training was going well, and everyone remained in good spirits. So Fred was naturally concerned when Will didn't turn up for training on the Thursday before the game. He asked Steve to try and get hold of him, and his worries grew when the player didn't answer his phone.

As training continued without him, rumours and conspiracy

theories started flying around as to Will's whereabouts. Initially, Fred gave him the benefit of the doubt, but come Friday, there was still no sign of him. Right midfielder Nelly Patterson knew Will better than anyone, having grown up together and shared the pitch at previous clubs. Fred summoned Nelly over after training.

'Nelly,' he said, putting his hand on the player's shoulder. 'I want you to find out what's happened to that mate of yours.'

'Got it, boss,' Nelly replied, nodding. 'Leave it to me.'

Later that afternoon, Fred's mobile started ringing. It was Nelly.

'Hi, boss,' Nelly began nervously. 'I haven't managed to find Will, but I've heard a rumour that he's disappeared off to a festival. I'd imagine it'll go on all weekend.'

Fred was apoplectic. 'A festival? He can't just swan off to a festival! You make sure he gets back for the game tomorrow!'

'But, boss...' Fred hung up before Nelly could finish.

Steam came out of Fred's ears. If Will hadn't been performing so well, the manager would've probably torn up his contract. But he knew the team stood little chance without him. So Fred decided to see if he'd turn up at the weekend before making any rash decisions.

⚽⚽⚽

Saturday arrived, and Fred waited nervously for the player to show up. Given everything Graham had been dealing with recently, Fred had chosen not to tell him about Will's disappearance. As members of the squad began arriving for the afternoon's fixture, Will was still nowhere to be seen.

Eventually, Graham walked past. 'You alright, Fred?' he asked. 'You look a bit stressed...'

Fred sighed resignedly. 'Um... yes, sort of. It's about Will...' Suddenly, he stopped in his tracks, spotting Will from the distance arriving with Nelly.

'Oh... nothing!' Fred continued, flustered.

Graham stared at Fred, eventually shrugging. Fred flashed a smile as Graham wandered off, before fixing his stare firmly towards Nelly and Will.

'Keep calm,' Fred told himself, as the two players approached. But his temper got the better of him. 'And where the bloody hell have you been?' Fred snapped, waving his arms at Will. 'You think you can just miss two days of training to go to a festival? What have you got to say for yourself?'

Will just looked at him blankly.

Nelly interjected, 'Um, boss, this isn't Will. Meet Gary — Will's identical twin brother.'

Gary awkwardly offered the manager his hand.

Fred was stunned. 'His brother?' he boomed. 'What is this? A family outing? Have you brought his granny along as well?'

Nelly unwisely sniggered. The manager glared at his player, before looking Gary up and down. Will's twin stood uneasily, his uncertain expression presenting a somewhat unimpressive sight.

'Besides, I didn't even know he had a twin?' Fred queried.

'Yeah,' Nelly explained, shifting apprehensively under his manager's scrutiny. 'I couldn't find Will anywhere, but managed to track down his twin, Gary. He's even better than Will. Could we play him for this game instead?'

Fred rolled his eyes. 'Haha. That's a good one. Don't you remember what happened with Tommy last month? He was supposed to be some kind of superstar. He'd never seen a football in his life!'

'C'mon, boss,' Nelly pleaded. 'It's not like that with Gary. Just see for yourself.'

Nelly signalled for Gary to showcase his football skills. Fred watched as he pinged three perfect shots into the top corner. Raising his eyebrow, Fred stared at Gary. This was someone who could clearly play football. But after the Tommy fiasco, he wanted to know more about this mystery twin.

'So tell me, Gary,' Fred said. 'Given you're obviously a good footballer, why aren't you already playing for someone else?'

'It's never been a great passion of mine,' Gary admitted. 'Don't get me wrong, I enjoy playing the odd game, and I know I'm pretty good. I just have other interests. But when Nelly told me that my brother had disappeared, I thought I could help you out.'

'Well, that's very noble of you,' Fred replied sarcastically. 'But it's too late. We'd never be able to register you in time.'

'Um, boss,' Nelly said quietly, avoiding his manager's eyes. 'He looks and sounds exactly like Will. Couldn't he just pretend to be him? No one would know.'

Fred's mind started racing. At the recent hearing, he and his chairman had sworn to the official — no more foul play. There was no way that Graham would agree to knowingly breaking the league's rules. But Nelly was right; Gary did look exactly like Will. Maybe they should just play him anyway? Graham would never have to find out...

As Fred pondered his next move, Gary grew increasingly unsettled.

'Nelly,' Gary said, frowning. 'I said I'd help out today as a favour for my brother. I never said I'd pretend to be him!'

'Relax, it'll be fine,' Nelly assured. 'No one apart from me even knows that you exist. You just have to pretend to be Will for 90 minutes, and that's it.' Nelly turned to his manager. 'What do you think?'

Fred stared into the distance, battling his conscience. After a period of soul-searching, he puffed out his cheeks and glanced between Nelly and Gary.

'OK,' Fred muttered, lowering his voice. 'But this stays strictly between the three of us. No one must ever know that you've pretended to be Will. Not the fans, not the players, not the opposition, and certainly not my chairman. Can you do that, Gary?'

Gary shifted uncomfortably. 'Um, yes... I suppose I can do it.'

'Great,' Fred replied, nodding at his new recruit. 'And remember, you're not Gary. You're Will!'

Gary nodded reluctantly, and the two players headed off to join the others for the warm-up.

The manager felt deeply uncomfortable going behind his

chairman's back. But what could he do? His team needed the points. As FC Farce's manager, it was his responsibility to do whatever it took to secure a result. And playing Gary gave them a much better chance of winning. He had no doubt that Will's identical twin could do a job for the team. What concerned him was whether Gary could keep up the act.

'Where've you been then, Will?' enquired Percy Plumb, as he applied his shin pads in the dressing room.

Gary coughed. 'Oh, I've just had a few days off. Personal reasons.'

Percy shrugged. 'Fair enough.' Fred exhaled in relief, turning his attention to the game ahead.

During Fred's final instructions, there was a sudden knock at the door. In walked the chairman. It was the first time he'd ever entered the dressing room before a match. His passionate words surprised everybody.

'Lads,' he began, with a smile that lit up the room. 'I'd just like to say thank you for all your efforts so far this season. I must admit, I wasn't completely thrilled at the prospect of becoming chairman. But over the last few weeks I've really enjoyed it. As long as we stick together and stay honest as a group, we'll be fine.'

These weren't just empty words. Despite his initial reluctance, Graham had grown unexpectedly fond of his new role. The camaraderie, the thrill of the matches, the passion of the fans — something had hooked him. Maybe, deep down, he even enjoyed the chaos that seemed to follow FC Farce like a shadow. It had dragged him well outside his comfort zone, but Graham had 'got' what owning a football club was all about.

As Graham beamed with pride at the group, Fred looked at the floor with guilt washing over him. He was unable to meet his chairman's eyes. Turning to leave the room, Graham had one final word.

'Good luck for today, lads. And Will, make sure your goalscoring run continues!'

Gary didn't say a word, just giving the chairman a weak thumbs-up. When Nelly asked him to step in for his brother, he had no idea he'd have to deceive everyone. As he stood in the tunnel and glanced at his oblivious teammates, Gary knew there was no turning back. All he could do was play his heart out.

As the whistle blew and the game kicked off, supporters chanted Will's name in appreciation of his recent goalscoring run. From the very beginning, Gary stamped his authority on the game. Within the first five minutes, he intercepted a pass near the halfway line. His agility allowed him to weave through the opposition midfield with ease. The other FC Farce players watched in awe of their teammate's newfound poise and skill.

The Worton defenders, expecting the erratic play they'd heard about from Will, were completely caught off guard by Gary's neat footwork. In the 10th minute, Gary's first significant contribution came when he received a long ball from midfielder Gavin O'Donnell. With a deft touch, he brought the ball under control and surged towards the penalty area. The defenders hesitated for a split second, and Gary unleashed a powerful shot that rattled the crossbar.

The fans were on their feet applauding. Although the ball didn't find the net, it was a clear statement of intent.

Worton United realised they were dealing with a different level of player to what they'd anticipated, and tightened up their defence. But the breakthrough came in the 35th minute. FC Farce won a corner, and as the ball was whipped in, Gary outjumped his marker and headed the ball towards goal. The goalkeeper made a spectacular save, but the rebound fell kindly to Nelly Patterson to easily slot home. The crowd erupted, crediting the goal to Will's persistence. Nelly celebrated the goal and gave a cheeky wink to Gary and his manager. Half-time came with FC Farce leading 1-0.

In the second half, Worton United pressed higher up the pitch, trying to disrupt FC Farce's rhythm. After 55 minutes their change of approach paid off, a defensive mix-up handing them an equaliser with a well-placed shot past Smithy.

Fred groaned at the setback, but remained confident. He instructed the team to be more direct and play the ball long to

'Will'. In the 75th minute, his moment of brilliance came. Receiving the ball just outside the penalty area, he charged towards goal and drew the attention of two defenders. He unselfishly laid the ball off to Matty Reynolds, who blasted it into the top corner. FC Farce were back in the lead.

The final 15 minutes were tense, with Worton United throwing everything forward in search of another equaliser. 'Great work, Will!' Fred cried, keeping up the act as Gary used his strength to relieve the mounting pressure.

Finally, the referee blew the final whistle, and FC Farce celebrated a hard-fought 2-1 victory. The fans, still blissfully unaware of the ruse, chanted Will's name in admiration. Gary's performance had been instrumental.

As the players celebrated with the fans, the chairman came down from the stands to congratulate the manager.

'Amazing!' Graham cooed. 'What a performance from the team. And what about Will? He was incredible out there. You and Steve have obviously done a great job with him in training.' Fred smiled weakly, with guilt washing over him again.

As his chairman went back up to the stands, Fred gestured for Gary to come over to the sidelines.

'So,' Fred asked in a low voice. 'Any chance someone might have figured it out?'

Gary shook his head. 'Don't think so.'

Fred nodded gratefully. 'Good. Listen, why don't you slip out early so you don't have to keep this up? I'll tell the guys you had to get back to your family. Thanks for today, by the way. You were immense.'

'Cool, no worries,' Gary replied. 'I actually really enjoyed that. If you're up for it, I'd definitely consider signing for the team properly — as myself this time!'

Fred looked at the player, forgetting all about his earlier guilt. Perhaps he could bring Gary back in January and introduce him properly as Will's twin? By then everyone would have forgotten all about this game, so Gary would be free to sign as a brand-new player. Then the twins could form a potentially lethal partnership and fire the team to safety. Yes, he really liked the sound of that...

Suddenly, Fred was interrupted from his daydream by Nelly rushing over. He looked concerned as he approached the pair.

'Um, boss...' Nelly said. 'The local media are down there. They want to interview Gary for Will's man of the match performance today.'

Gary's eyes widened. 'I can't do that! I get nervous in front of a camera. I'll slip up.'

Fred grabbed hold of the player. 'Look, Gary, it'll be suspicious if you don't speak to them. Just relax, you'll be fine. Stick to short answers and don't go off on a tangent. I'll come over with you.'

Gary looked visibly sick. But there was no time to back out, as the cameraman had already spotted the player and beckoned him over. Fred looked at Gary and mouthed that it would all be OK, and the pair went off to face the media. Gary greeted the interviewer with a nervous handshake.

The camera started rolling. 'Wow! Congratulations, Will,' the interviewer exclaimed. 'You took your performance to a new level today. Where did that come from?'

Incredibly, Will's twin played his second blinder of the day. 'To be honest, it's all been down to hard work,' bluffed Gary. 'I've been doing extra work in training, and today it really showed. This result isn't down to me, it's down to the staff and the coaches who have put their time and effort into me. I can't thank them enough.'

Fred gave him a silent thumbs-up, and Gary continued answering the questions with confidence. He even cheekily said that this performance had come from 'the new Will'! As the interviewer switched off his camera and left, Fred stared at Gary in awe.

'Wow, fair play, Gary,' he gasped. 'That was a great interview. Now you get going. Give it a few months and I'll get in touch about signing permanently. Let all this die down a bit first.'

Gary shook Fred's hand, and off he went, greeting some young fans on the way out. By now Fred didn't feel an ounce of guilt for what had happened. He'd taken a risk and it had paid off big time. The team were happy, Graham was happy, the fans were happy — everyone was happy. If Will finally returned, he just needed to make sure he didn't reveal the truth!

⚽⚽⚽

As Fred headed into training Monday morning, he wondered if Will would be back from the festival. Arriving at the training ground, there was still no sign of him. *Oh well, no loss*, he thought. But Fred was surprised to see Graham waiting for him. The usually mild-mannered chairman looked seriously angry.

Fred immediately feared the worst, but painted on a smile. 'Hi, chairman,' he said brightly.

'Oh, morning, Fred,' Graham replied sarcastically. 'Let me ask you something. Were you ever going to tell me that Will had a twin?'

Fred froze as his chairman angrily gave him the full lowdown. After pulling off a series of blinders, Gary made one error that proved to be fatal. One of the young fans he greeted asked for his autograph. Gary happily obliged and accidentally signed his real name. The young lad was a Worton United supporter, and his eagle-eyed father noticed the mystery name 'Gary'. After doing some digging on the internet, the dad discovered the truth and reported the club to the football league.

'So yeah, thanks, mate,' Graham spat, rolling his eyes. 'We've got to go back and see that football league official tomorrow. I'm sure he'll be pleased to see us again.'

With that the chairman stormed off. As Fred desperately tried to call him back, the real Will finally returned. The player had a spring in his step, seemingly without a care in the world.

'The wanderer returns,' Fred muttered sarcastically. 'Tell me, Will, how was the festival?'

Will raised an eyebrow. 'Festival? I haven't been to a festival. I injured my testicle. I've been having minor surgery. Didn't you get my message?'

Fred froze for the second time in two minutes. 'You've been injured?'

'Yep, I'm fine now though,' said Will cheerily. 'Just needed to rest for a couple of days. How did we do on Saturday?'

The manager buried his head in his hands. Nelly Patterson's 'festival' rumour had obviously been misheard. Forget testicle — Fred's gamble had well and truly bitten him on the arse.

CHAPTER 5

OCTOBER – FEELING SHEEPISH

'Oh, nice to see you again, gentlemen,' the football league official quipped, with mock surprise. 'It seems FC Farce has a knack for finding itself in, how should I put it... *farcical situations*.' He looked pleased with that one.

Graham's face flushed with embarrassment. Fred stared intently at the floor, with guilt etched across his face. Here they were, for the second time in less than a month, hauled in front of the league committee like naughty schoolboys.

The official put on a stern face and continued. 'This time, the issue is very serious. It has come to our attention that FC Farce knowingly fielded an ineligible player in last week's match against Worton United. This is a blatant violation of league rules.'

Fred tensed, sensing what was coming next.

'Due to this breach, the committee has no choice but to dock FC Farce three points, effectively cancelling your victory. And the player Gary Watkins, who I understand knowingly posed as his twin brother, is banned from participating in the league for the next three years.'

A stunned silence filled the room. Graham glared angrily at Fred, his fists clenched by his sides. Shuffling his papers, the official leaned forward for a final warning.

'Gentlemen, I do hope this will be the last time we meet under such unfortunate circumstances. I trust FC Farce will adhere strictly to the rules from now on.' With a dismissive wave, he ushered the two men towards the exit.

Once outside, Graham didn't look at Fred. He stared down at his shoes, the earlier pride he'd felt in his new role replaced by a knot of disappointment and anger. It wasn't about the lost points — it was the feeling of betrayal. Fred had gone behind his back, and Graham could barely contain his anger. He didn't say a word; he simply turned and walked off.

For the first two league games in October, the chairman stayed away altogether. He missed a credible 1-1 draw at home to Retton United — where the away fans took great delight in singing, 'Where's your striker gone?' — and a 3-0 away defeat to Nelton Rovers.

The only bright spot was a comfortable 3-0 win against Kifferton Town in the first round of the Combinations Cup. Kifferton were two divisions below FC Farce and fancied their chances, so the team were relieved to come through unscathed. But the chairman wasn't there to see it.

For Fred, the verdict had more than a twinge of unfortunate irony. The points deduction was bad enough, but Gary's three-year ban was a real choker. Thanks to the misjudged gamble, bringing him back in January was a non-starter. He felt bad for Gary. After all, he hadn't wanted to be in the situation in the first place. Meanwhile, the real Will Watkins found the whole situation greatly amusing.

'Will I be credited for my brother's man of the match performance?' he quipped, struggling to contain his laughter.

At the training ground, Fred paced the edge of the touchline with his hands firmly in his pockets. Every time he thought of Graham's empty seat in the stands, a pang of regret knotted in his stomach. He cursed himself for going behind his chairman's back. Especially when Graham was just starting to enjoy his new role.

All I can do is keep trying to get results for this football club, he eventually thought to himself, attempting to bat his inner guilt away. *Graham will be back before long...*

With the chairman distancing himself from the day-to-day running of the club, FC Farce's admin operations began slipping. One simmering issue was an ongoing feud with a local farmer called Ned Thompson. Ned's farm bordered the stadium grounds, and he was getting increasingly irate about fans parking on his fields and trampling over his land on matchdays.

Inspecting the latest damage left from the Retton United game, farmer Ned decided enough was enough. He dialled the number of the club's head office, hoping to be put through to somebody in charge. The phone rang and rang before finally being picked up by Old Bill, the hapless kit man. He answered the phone with a loud yawn.

'Who's this?'

'Hello, this is Ned Thompson,' came the firm voice on the other end of the line. 'I own the farm next to the stadium. I've called several times about fans parking on my land and causing damage, but nothing's been done. I need to speak to the chairman.'

Old Bill let out a long, deliberate sigh. 'Hold on, let me see if I can find someone.'

Putting the receiver down, he shuffled aimlessly around the office for a few moments, muttering under his breath. Ned's grip on the phone tightened.

Eventually, Old Bill responded. 'The chairman's not around right now. In fact, nobody is! Could you call back another time?'

Ned's patience was running out. 'Look, I've called countless times. This is serious. My fields are getting ruined. Can't you at least take a message?'

'Fine... fine,' Old Bill replied slowly, fumbling around for a pen. 'What's the message?'

Ned took a deep breath, trying to keep his cool. 'Tell the chairman that if this isn't sorted out soon, I'll be taking matters into my own hands.'

Old Bill scribbled something on a piece of paper. 'Got it,' he said, not attempting to hide a yawn. 'I'll pass it on. Goodbye.' As soon as he ended the call, he stuffed the note in his pocket and forgot all about it.

Ned hung up the phone, trembling with anger. Given the disinterest from the man he'd just spoken to, he doubted his message would even make it past the desk, let alone reach the chairman. And sure enough, after the cup game against Kifferton Town, Ned found his fields littered with waste and destroyed. He stood at the edge of the field, studying his ruined land with his arms folded. He kicked at a pile of discarded rubbish, his inner rage reaching boiling point.

Enough was enough.

⚽⚽⚽

The club's next league game was at home to Zacton Rovers. The opponents were just above FC Farce in the table, so it was a crucial match in the battle for survival. It was a crisp autumn afternoon, and the match was a complete sell-out.

Squinting towards the stands, Fred hoped this might be the game that Graham returned after his spell of absence. But as the players took the field, Fred noticed the chairman's usual seat was still empty. He felt a sudden twinge of disappointment, but immediately put it out of his mind to focus on the match.

Despite the off-field issues, things seemed to click on the pitch. From the first whistle, FC Farce took control. Central midfielder Gavin O'Donnell was having by far his best game for the club, dictating play and running the show in the middle of the park. He threaded a perfect through ball to Will's strike partner Percy Plumb, who for once took the shot on early, slotting the ball home to make it 1-0.

The crowd were on their feet applauding. On the sidelines, Fred was mightily impressed with the well-taken finish.

'Keep it up, lads!' he encouraged, clapping enthusiastically.

As the first half wore on, FC Farce continued to dominate and make life difficult for their opponents. Nelly Patterson was causing havoc on the right-hand side of midfield, while Percy Plumb was a constant menace after his goal. The defence, led by the fit again Clive Harrison and Barry McGraw, were comfortably keeping the Zacton Rovers attackers at bay.

When the half-time whistle came, the team came off to a standing ovation. With the way the team were playing, it seemed inevitable that FC Farce would add to their lead in the second half.

Little did anyone know; trouble was brewing just outside the stadium.

Consumed by mounting fury, farmer Ned Thompson had carefully plotted his revenge. As the second half kicked off, Ned and a team of farmers loaded up trailers with hundreds of sheep. With military precision, they manoeuvred the convoy to the edge of the pitch.

One of the four sides of the stadium was completely open, leaving the farmers with a free rein to move into position. The supporters watched open-mouthed as the convoy plotted its final move. The players and the referee were also visibly distracted by the unusual events.

On the sidelines, Fred froze mid-stride. 'What the hell is going on over there?' he exclaimed, staring towards the spectacle. Once the penny dropped, his eyes widened in horror, bracing himself for what was about to unfold.

Finally, the farmers opened the gates and hundreds of sheep poured onto the pitch. The place descended into mayhem. Sheep charged towards the terrified players, bleating hysterically and going absolutely berserk. One player dodged to the side, nearly colliding with a sheep that had charged at him full force.

Petrified fans shrieked, scrambling for the exits. The bleating grew louder as more of the flock galloped onto the pitch, hooves clattering against the turf. The sharp scent of panic and manure filled the air as sheep darted in every direction, tearing the ground to shreds.

'Could all the pitch invaders please leave the field,' the stadium announcer jokingly asked, in a misjudged move.

The surreal sight of crazed animals running amok, leaving a path of destruction in their wake was a new level of madness, even for FC Farce. It was complete and utter bedlam.

There was no way the match could continue. The game was unofficially abandoned, with the referee having already bolted from the stadium and unavailable to make the official call.

'C'mon, get in here!' Fred shrieked, ushering his players towards the safety of the dressing room.

Inside, the cowering players sat pale and wide-eyed, some exchanging confused glances while others simply sat in stunned silence. Fred paced furiously, trying to make sense of it all. *What on earth had just happened?* He figured it must have been a bizarre prank, maybe a crazed away fan's idea of a sick joke. Thank goodness Graham hadn't been around to witness the latest disaster.

Meanwhile, Ned Thompson defiantly stood by his trailer, arms crossed with a look of grim satisfaction on his face. He'd made his point in the most spectacular way possible.

The aftermath was predictably hysterical. The local media couldn't believe their luck, the headline: 'Ewe Won't Believe The Latest Farce!' plastered over the back pages. With his head firmly buried in his hands, Fred received a call from the football league official.

'Good game, was it?' he quipped. 'Look, I'm letting you know that we're going to spare you the dubious honour of attending FC Farce's third hearing in less than three months. Frankly, we're fed up with the sight of you.'

'Thanks, I think?' Fred muttered, rolling his eyes.

'But you can tell that chairman of yours to get his house in order. Oh, one other thing. The result will naturally be awarded to your opponents...'

Fred angrily slammed down the phone and loudly swore. This latest points deduction saw FC Farce slump to the foot of the table. Another kick in the teeth.

Meanwhile, the AWOL chairman first heard the news of the sheep invasion shortly after the match. He spat out his tea in horror as he watched the early evening news, witnessing dozens of demented animals charging around his stadium. Recovering his composure, he reached for his phone, his head spinning with questions.

When he heard about the farmer situation, a pang of guilt twisted in his stomach. *I should have been there,* he thought of travelling fans let their feelings known, angrily booing the players and shouting obscenities.

The air in the dressing room was thick with the stench of sweat and defeat. Percy Plumb sat hunched on the bench, staring at his untied boots, while Nelly Patterson ran a hand through his damp hair. Fred stood at the front, hands hanging limply by his sides, staring at the floor. He opened his mouth to speak, but for once, no words came out. The manner of the defeat had completely drained him.

For Graham, back watching from the stands, the result was a bitter pill to swallow. The team had ruined any chance of a much-needed cash injection. With the club's finances already severely stretched, he had no idea how they'd sort out the situation with Ned Thompson.

The following week, as Graham winced at a mounting pile of bills, his phone suddenly rang. It was the football league official. The chairman instantly felt a twinge of dread.

'Um, Graham Farce here,' he answered tentatively, pacing the room.

'Hello, Mr Farce. I have some good news for a change,' the official began.

The official explained that, according to league rules, any victory by six or more goals triggered an obligatory drugs test for a random selection of the winning team's players. Nelton Rovers knew this was only procedure and happily obliged with the test. But one of their players had returned irregular findings.

Graham didn't dare pre-empt what was coming next. 'So... what does it mean?' he demanded, trembling with excitement.

'It means that Nelton Rovers have been disqualified from the competition,' the official replied matter-of-factly. 'So despite your team's crushing defeat, FC Farce will advance to the next round. Congratulations.'

Graham punched the air in delight, too elated to care about the official's sarcasm. The stunning news was just the lift he needed.

The news was met with a mix of disbelief and hilarity by

everyone else at the club. Fred, still reeling from the weekend's miserable defeat, could hardly believe his luck. The players were equally dumbfounded.

The irony was, if FC Farce *hadn't* been so woeful on Saturday and lost by fewer goals, the obligatory test would never have happened!

Graham stood before the players, his face alight with excitement. 'We've been given an incredible lifeline, let's make the most of it!' He gave a sly grin. 'And if we *do* end up losing in the third round, make sure it's by at least six goals so they have to do another test!'

On the day of the third round draw, the club was buzzing with excitement. To mark the occasion, Fred invited everyone over to his house to watch the draw and learn their next opponents.

The chairman, players, coaches, and several club staff joined Fred to huddle around his small television. As the clock ticked closer to the start, the packed living room fell silent with anticipation, praying that the draw wouldn't be another anticlimax.

'Here we go!' exclaimed Graham, as the big moment finally arrived.

Just as the first tie was about to be revealed, the TV went black, and all the lights went out. A collective groan filled the room as a power cut plunged them into darkness.

'Typical,' muttered Fred, shaking his head in frustration. Graham tried his mobile phone, but there was no signal at Fred's remote countryside home.

The room was up in arms. 'What the hell do we do now?' Right back Ollie Wright cried.

Fred's managerial instincts kicked in. 'Right, lads, we need to find some signal. Who's up for a run up the hill?'

Without hesitation, Will Watkins sprang to his feet. 'I'll do it!' he said, already heading for the door.

His teammates watched with amusement as Will sprinted out of the house and disappeared into the darkness. Given his unpredictability, the rest of the group wondered if he'd even come back. Time seemed to crawl by as they waited for the player to return, with minutes passing by like hours. Finally, he burst back into the room, out of breath but grinning wildly.

'Well, who is it?' Fred demanded.

Will took a deep breath. 'Haverstone United, away!'

A stunned silence fell, then the whole room erupted into wild cheers. Haverstone United were three divisions higher than FC Farce, one of the biggest clubs in the competition. While the scale of the task was daunting, the chairman's prayers for a much-needed cash injection had been answered.

'Cheers!' Graham grinned, clinking his glass of beer with Fred's.

CHAPTER 6

NOVEMBER – CUP FEVER

'Next Thursday at 7:30pm, live on the Football Tonight radio show?' Graham repeated back to the voice on the phone, frantically checking his calendar. 'Erm, yes... I think I can make that. Speak then.'

Crossing the date off, Graham slumped in his office chair, letting out a long, deliberate sigh. His phone had been ringing off the hook with messages from national reporters. The intense scrutiny was a far cry from the relatively sleepy local coverage. Naturally, the chairman was delighted with the draw and the prospect of raising some decent funds. But the size of the challenge ahead soon hit home.

Later, he looked into his manager's eyes. 'What do you make of our chances then, honestly?'

Staring back at his chairman, Fred pulled no punches. 'Put it this way... I'll be delighted if we get away with losing by single figures.'

'Ah. That's the spirit.'

Before worrying about keeping the score down, the club quickly had to come up with a fair way of allocating tickets. With the immense reaction to the draw, Graham knew that nearly the entire population of Henlon would be after tickets.

'So how can we do this?' he asked his admin team. Initially, Graham was met with a stony silence.

Eventually, no-nonsense team leader Doris stood up. 'Quite frankly, it's going to be hell,' she said, placing her hands on her hips. 'We've only got a small team as it is.'

'I know,' Graham replied, briefly pausing for thought. 'To keep it fair for everyone, we'll have to sell tickets both online and in-person at the ticket office.'

'Well, it's going to have to be all hands on deck then,' replied Doris. 'Everyone's going to have to help out.'

Graham's expression flickered. 'What, even…'

'Yes, even Old Bill,' Doris said firmly.

Graham shuddered, but eventually nodded in agreement.

On the morning of the ticket release, Graham paced up and down in his office intently. His big concern was the website's ability to keep up with the online orders. The website had been built several years ago on a shoestring budget and had never been upgraded. It would be a huge ask for the clunky system to cope. As the release time drew closer, Graham could hardly speak.

Unsurprisingly, the website failed at the first hurdle. *'What's happening?'* he cried at FC Farce's IT manager.

'It's crashed,' he replied, looking dazed. 'The traffic has brought it to a standstill.'

Graham watched helplessly as the IT manager struggled to get the creaking system back up and running. But it was no good. They were forced to abandon website orders completely, much to the anger of everyone trying to secure tickets online. Meanwhile, the line of eager fans camped at the ticket office continued to grow, with club staff scrambling behind the scenes to restore order.

Frustration grew throughout the long queue outside the ticket office. Fans shifted their weight from one foot to the other, glancing irritably at their watches. Near the front, one man slammed his hands against the barrier.

'What the hell is taking so long?' he barked, his voice carrying through the crowd. Old Bill, oblivious to the tension, cheerily hummed and continued scribbling names at a snail's pace.

Some fans attempted to push in, resulting in further confrontations and the odd scuffle. Graham attempted to calm things down by assuring the crowd they'd all be served eventually, but his voice was drowned out by the baying mob.

At one point, a gust of wind blew some of the tickets off the makeshift desk, sending them fluttering into the air like confetti.

A mad scramble ensued, which nearly turned into a mass riot, with fans fighting amongst themselves to grab the free tickets. It took several stewards to eventually wrestle them back from their grasp.

At the end of the day, many fans left empty-handed and disgruntled, while others were unsure if their names had even been recorded correctly. Not to mention all the fans who'd missed out trying to purchase online.

Addressing his worn-out admin staff, Graham put his hands up. 'That simply wasn't good enough,' he told them, shaking his head intently. 'Mark my words, upgrading that shoddy system will be my number one priority.'

Doris, tired and fed up, silently nodded in acknowledgement. The only one who seemed satisfied with the day's events was Old Bill — apparently oblivious to the chaos that had unfolded around him. He left the ticket office cheerily whistling after a 'successful day's work' while the rest of the staff shook their heads in bemusement.

Graham sighed ruefully. 'At least we can focus on the game now.'

⚽⚽⚽

In the cramped office, Fred and his coaching team watched clips of Haverstone United, flinching as they witnessed their vastly superior opponents in action. They didn't have many weaknesses.

Steve squinted, looking for something to latch onto. 'Their centre backs are... um, pretty short,' he said slowly. 'And their left back, well, he's not exactly the quickest.'

Fred nodded. 'So, we need to get the ball out to Nelly Patterson on the right,' he decided. 'Maybe his pace can cause some problems.' He paused, scratching his chin. 'Trouble is, he can't cross to save his life...'

Turning to his first team coach, Fred grinned. 'Over to you, Steve!'

At training the next day, Steve beckoned the player over. 'Alright, Nelly,' he said, pointing towards the cones and goalposts set up on the pitch. 'Today, we're focusing on crossing. If we're going to have any chance against Haverstone, we need to get you whipping the ball into the box.'

Nelly gave him a thumbs-up, but looked apprehensive. Dribbling past defenders was his bread and butter, but crossing was a different beast entirely. On his first attempt, Nelly sped down the line, leaving the imaginary defenders in his wake. He reached the crossing position, swung his foot, and sent the ball soaring high over the goal and into the empty stands. Steve watched the ball disappear into the distance.

'Alright, Nelly, let's try again. This time, focus on keeping the ball lower,' Steve advised.

Nelly nodded, visibly concentrating. He repeated the run, reached the crossing point, and kicked the ball. This time it stayed low, but far too low, skimming the grass and barely making it past the penalty area. It rolled harmlessly away from danger. Remembering his earlier success with Will, Steve remained undeterred.

'Better, but we need more lift,' Steve encouraged. 'Think of it like a sweet spot — not too high, not too low.'

Nelly paused to compose himself, wiping the sweat from his forehead. The next drill involved Steve acting as a striker. Nelly's task was to deliver the ball precisely to Steve's head. After a few more wayward crosses, one hitting Steve square in the face and leaving him momentarily dazed, Nelly finally managed a decent cross that Steve could head towards the goal.

'Much better!' Steve exclaimed, recovering from the facial assault and giving Nelly a thumbs-up.

Gradually, Nelly's crosses improved. They were still inconsistent, with some flying into the bushes and others skimming the ground, but every now and then, he managed a clean delivery.

When he rejoined his team, Fred strolled over, raising an eyebrow at Steve. 'How'd he do?'

Steve shrugged. 'Still pretty inconsistent,' he admitted. 'But there's some progress.'

Fred sighed, glancing across the field. 'Look, it's probably not going to change the outcome,' he said. 'But we've got to try something.'

The following Saturday, as the players trudged off the freezing pitch after yet another defeat, Fred's concerns hit a new low. Biting away shivers, the manager reflected on November's dismal run of form. This latest loss left FC Farce rooted to the foot of the table. Glancing at the scoreboard, he couldn't shake the idea that the looming cup tie had stolen their focus.

The more he thought about it, the more the Haverstone United game filled him with dread. A heavy cup defeat could destroy the team's fragile confidence.

As the big match approached, Fred put his fears to one side, painting on a broad smile as he began the pre-match press conference. The first question came from a cheeky young journalist.

'Fred, congratulations on progressing to round three after the 7-0 defeat to Nelton Rovers. Do you think your team stands a chance tomorrow?'

Ignoring the sarcasm, Fred cleared his throat. 'Well, football is a funny old game, isn't it? Anything can happen on the day. We're going to give it our all.'

A tabloid journalist piped up next, eager to get a bite from the manager. 'Fred, do you think you might need a miracle to get past Haverstone United? Or are you hoping for another sheep invasion to distract them?'

Fred's eyes narrowed slightly, but he kept his composure. 'We've been working on a few things in training. We'll be ready.'

Another smirking reporter couldn't resist a further dig. 'Fred, given all the goings-on at your club this year, is there a chance of an actual football match breaking out tomorrow, or will it just be another farce?'

Finally, Fred's patience snapped. 'Listen, we know we've had our ups and downs this season,' he said sharply. 'But the lads are ready to give everything. I think we'll leave the questions there.'

With that, the manager stormed out of the press conference. He could tell by the looks on everyone's faces that they expected nothing less than a thrashing for his team. Deep down, he shared that view. But he was determined for FC Farce not to become a complete laughingstock.

⚽⚽⚽

That night, the players and management all went to bed early, bracing themselves for the 250-mile trek to Haverstone. Tossing and turning, Graham was haunted by visions of his players oversleeping and missing the bus entirely. So when he saw everyone gathered and ready at dawn, he breathed a huge sigh of relief. The long journey south began with everyone in good spirits.

Almost immediately, things went wrong. The driver, cut from the same cloth as Old Bill, didn't seem to have a clue where he was going. He started muttering that he'd misplaced his map.

'I know it's around here somewhere,' he mumbled.

He started rifling through his pockets, before triumphantly unfolding an enormous paper map that completely blocked the windscreen.

'You can't drive with that man!' Graham cried, lunging forward just as the bus swerved wildly.

Several players rushed to help as the bus wobbled from side to side. Eventually, they managed to peel the map away from the driver's hands. But the commotion hadn't gone unnoticed — attracting the attention of a local policeman who happened to be driving past. He suspected something was off and immediately pulled the vehicle.

The officer climbed aboard and took in the scene with an incredulous look. 'Everything alright here, gentlemen?'

Graham attempted a disarming smile. 'Yes, officer. All under control!'

Ignoring him, the policeman stared straight at the driver. 'Now tell me,' he enquired. 'Can you please explain what caused you to drive so erratically?'

'It was... the map,' the driver stammered, dazed and disoriented.

'The map!' the policeman shrieked. 'What on earth are you

talking about? You're telling me a map made you drive like that? I don't know what you've taken today, but you're clearly in no fit state to be behind the wheel!'

'No, no!' Graham cried, throwing up his arms in protest. 'We can explain.'

Too late. The policeman ordered everybody off the coach. He insisted on breathalysing the driver, and when the result showed no hint of intoxication, breathalysing every single person on the coach. As one negative result after another came back, the officer's face tightened in irritation.

'So it appears everybody is sober,' he eventually said wearily, raising his eyebrow. 'Can someone tell me what's going on then?'

Graham and Fred desperately tried to explain the driver's struggles with his oversized map. With a heavy sigh, the policeman eventually shook his head.

'Alright, alright,' he said, pushing out his hand. 'That's quite enough. Look, this is wasting my time. I'm going to let you off with a warning. Just be more careful next time, eh?'

Graham exhaled in relief. 'Yes, of course. Thank you, officer.'

But the encounter set the tone for the journey ahead. Without his map, the driver was pretty much clueless again. After another hour of driving around aimlessly, he finally admitted to the group, 'Uh... I think we're lost.'

'Lost?' Fred cried. 'How can we be lost? Just keep heading south!'

They drove in circles, missed turns, and ended up on backroads. Eventually they got back on track, but had wasted several hours going the wrong way. To make matters worse, the traffic was heaving. As the minutes ticked by, the manager and chairman grew more anxious about whether they'd make it in time.

Then an hour before kick-off, still several miles from the stadium, the bus gave a violent splutter and shuddered to a halt. Graham let his head fall against the seat. 'What now?'

The driver shrugged helplessly. 'Uh... I think we broke down.'

Graham's eyes closed. 'Terrific.'

Panic set in as Graham frantically made contact with Haverstone

United, desperately trying to explain the situation. They were less than sympathetic to FC Farce's plight.

'Look, I don't care what's happened,' the Haverstone official snapped, adopting a serious superiority complex. 'If you're not here in 30 minutes, you forfeit the match.'

Graham kicked the floor in frustration. It was déjà vu from the pre-season friendly earlier in the season, but this time far worse. Not only would the club lose out on the vital gate receipts, they'd receive embarrassment and unwanted attention on a national scale. Plus, a significant fine and an inevitable third football league hearing.

'What are we going to tell the fans?' Graham cried, staring bleakly at the stalled bus. Fred, meanwhile, was already imagining the smug look on that reporter's face from the press conference.

'Those smarmy reporters will love it if we forfeit this game,' he muttered.

Just as everyone gave up hope, a lorry pulled over. A tall, burly man climbed out and approached them. The only trouble was, he was an Eastern European gentleman who hardly spoke any English. Fred attempted to take control of the situation.

'You hurt your foot?' the man asked, looking confused.

'No, I haven't hurt my foot,' Fred said, waving his arms. 'We are here to play football. Foot... ball.'

'You want to sell me football?' the man replied, scratching his head.

After several excruciating minutes, the message seemed to get through that they needed to be at Haverstone United's stadium for a football match as quickly as possible.

The man grinned. 'I help you!' He motioned towards his oversized vehicle.

The moment everyone piled into the back of the lorry, the smell hit them — oil, metal, and something that might have been stale cabbage. As the group collectively questioned their sanity, the engine roared to life.

The first jolt sent the players flying into one another. The lorry lurched again, hurling them towards the other side like clothes in a washing machine. The walls rattled as they tore down the road, each bump and pothole feeling like a minor earthquake.

Graham, wedged between two players, leaned towards Fred. 'Are we heading for Haverstone... or Romania?' he quipped, barely keeping his balance. The minutes slowly ticked by.

After what felt like an eternity, the lorry slowed. There was a collective intake of breath as it shuddered to a halt. The back doors creaked open, and sunlight streamed in, momentarily blinding them. Fred squinted and leaned forward, his heart pounding in his chest. Were they anywhere near civilisation?

Graham clambered to the front, blinking against the light. The large sign read: *'Welcome to Haverstone United.'*

'Thank God!' Graham cried. They'd made it with minutes to spare.

The home fans watched in amazement as their unknown opposition rocked up in the back of a lorry, driven by a bewildered Eastern European. Learning the circumstances behind their arrival, everyone found it hilarious, giving the whole team a loud cheer as they finally entered the stadium. Meanwhile, the unlikely chauffeur named Timo was declared as the afternoon's unofficial guest of honour.

The incident seemed to take the sting out of the occasion. Ahead of the match, Fred was more relaxed than usual.

'Look, lads, if there was any pressure, it's completely disappeared now,' he said, laughing. 'Haverstone United probably think we're a bunch of lunatics. There's nothing to lose — just enjoy it!'

For the second time that season, Graham also made an appearance in the dressing room. 'Lads, I'm sorry about the bus breaking down. I'll add it to my never-ending list of things to fix,' he joked. 'Like your manager said, just enjoy it out there today.'

Fred's strategy was simple. Get the ball out to Nelly Patterson to get crosses in the box. Midway through the first half, Fred and his coaching staff looked on in stunned silence as the right midfielder dribbled past the opposition left back and whipped in a perfect ball. Time seemed to stand still as Will Watkins rose above the centre backs, leaping like a salmon to head home the opening goal.

The Haverstone United supporters were gobsmacked. FC Farce had taken the lead!

Fred leapt into the air, disbelief and joy colliding as he and his coaches erupted on the touchline. For a brief moment, euphoria swept away the weight of their season's struggles. Graham celebrated more wildly than he'd ever celebrated before. The travelling fans exploded in pandemonium, momentarily daring to dream of a historic upset.

Eventually, Haverstone's class showed. They ran out 3-1 winners against their lower league opponents. But FC Farce battled valiantly, with Percy Plumb missing a golden opportunity to make things interesting with a few minutes to go.

At full-time the whole ground rose to give FC Farce a standing ovation. On the touchline, Fred rigorously clapped his hands and beamed with pride. FC Farce were beaten, but for once they'd gained the respect of their opponents. After turning up in the back of a lorry, that was an achievement in itself.

The press were far more complimentary after the match. The same journalist who'd previously ridiculed their chances begged Fred for an interview, gushing over FC Farce's spirited performance.

Fred smirked. 'That's quite a change of heart from yesterday...'

Meanwhile, Graham was overjoyed with the team's brave efforts, the image of Will's opening goal vividly playing out in his mind.

'Dad would have loved that moment,' he told Fred with a broad smile.

With the coach fixed, the sound of laughter and clinking beer bottles filled the air as the group reflected on the day's events. And with intense concentration, the driver finally managed to get the hang of the route home.

Bidding his players farewell, Fred felt a warm glow. Rather than damaging their confidence, the mishap had done wonders in lifting everybody's spirits. The latest farce was deemed as a successful one.

Thanks, Timo, Fred thought to himself. *You'll go down as a hero alongside our Japanese friend Tommy.*

CHAPTER 7

DECEMBER – SILENT NIGHT

The Haverstone United game temporarily gave Fred renewed confidence. With FC Farce back in league action just three days later, Fred urged his players to take the spirit they'd shown at Haverstone into their battle to stay up. They were still rock bottom, with the gap slowly widening.

The team played two league games in quick succession — losing both. Fred's optimism was shattered as they were beaten at Brackington Town on a freezing Tuesday night, followed by a 4-0 hammering at home to Killerton Rovers.

Following the Killerton game, as the team trudged off with their heads stooped low, angry FC Farce fans jeered them for their perceived lack of effort. The toxic atmosphere was a stark contrast to the previous Saturday at Haverstone, where the fans had applauded the team's heroics so warmly.

'Jesus, a week is a long time in football,' Fred muttered as he followed his players into the solitude of the dressing room.

As Fred watched the lads limp through their next training session, the evidence was plain to see. They were all bloody knackered. No matter what he tried — whether that was encouraging, shouting, or waving his arms — his fallen cup heroes looked lost and devoid of confidence.

'And what about Nelly, eh?' he exclaimed to coach Steve. 'Ever since he popped the ball onto Will's head at Haverstone, he's been absolutely useless!'

'I know,' replied Steve, shaking his head vigorously. 'It's like he's forgotten everything we worked on.'

The cup adventure had created wonderful memories, not to

mention paying off the irate farmer. But in hindsight, it might have been an unwelcome distraction after all.

Speaking of unwelcome distractions, Christmas party season was fast approaching. Graham grimaced as he recalled stories of parties from Trevor's tenure. His father's quirky personality ensured some memorable events — usually for all the wrong reasons.

One year, Trevor got drunk and left early, accidentally locking everyone in the club's boardroom for the night. With nothing but alcohol to keep them entertained, the group looked a sorry sight when a startled morning cleaning lady finally set them free. The players still felt the effects in their next match several days later, one being physically sick all over the pitch. They were hammered 6-0.

Other festive bashes resulted in frolics and fisticuffs, and the occasional moony pulled at unsuspecting traffic. Such misdemeanours present a golden opportunity for the local press to catch the team misbehaving. This prospect gave Graham nightmares. As the football league official told him earlier, they'd hit the headlines enough that season.

Something that nearly every Christmas party had in common was excessive alcohol intake. Graham's infamous fans' forum performance showed that he enjoyed a beer every now and then. But as he shuddered at the thought of his players being splashed across the local back pages, he was determined to keep things under control.

'Right everyone, this is how it goes,' Graham warned, glancing sternly at his coaching team. 'At the Christmas party, there will be no excessive drinking, no drunken silliness, and certainly no afterparties. But I do want everyone to enjoy themselves…'

The assembled group raised their eyebrows. 'Thanks, chairman, really looking forward to this…'

'Glad to hear it,' Graham replied bluntly, ignoring the sarcasm. 'Fred, I'll leave you to tell the players about the plans.'

'Thanks again, Graham,' Fred muttered.

With that, Graham left them to it. Watching the chairman go

safely out of view, Coach Steve glanced at Fred and frowned.

'Why do we have to watch our drinking?' Steve moaned, as if the chairman had asked him to scrub his toilet. 'We're not the ones playing football.'

Fred subtly concurred with a knowing nod.

Graham's stance was simple — everyone should play by the same rules. Besides, his father's Christmas parties had taught him that often the coaching team behaved worse than the players!

'Any luck, Doris?' Graham later asked hopefully, peering into the tatty admin office.

'Nope. Fully booked.'

Graham sighed. Thanks to the club's ongoing chaos, organising the Christmas party had been pushed to the back of the priority list. Now in December, finding a venue was proving challenging, threatening to derail the festivities before they even started.

Watching Doris slam the phone down after yet another rejection, Graham made an executive decision. The party would be held at the stadium. He gave the green light for a giant marquee to be erected on the pitch, complete with a dance floor and stage for live music.

Plus, Graham was good friends with the lead singer of a local band who owed him a favour, so it wouldn't be too expensive.

'What do you think, guys?' he said to his staff, after revealing the grand plans.

The reaction was different this time. 'To be honest, that actually sounds pretty decent, Graham.'

Graham was pleased. Despite the excessive drink warnings, his staff were finally showing some enthusiasm about the occasion.

⚽⚽⚽

First up, the team had the small matter of an important bottom-of-the-table clash. Despite their poor run of form, FC Farce were only two points behind their next home opponents Vickington Town. It was a freezing cold Friday night game, but there was a red-hot atmosphere as the teams entered the pitch. A win would move FC Farce off the foot of the table. Meanwhile, Vickington Town's large vocal following defied the December weather, determined to see their team widen the gap further.

From the moment the referee's whistle blew, it was clear the game wasn't going to be a classic. The teams were bottom two for a reason. It was a tough watch played in bitterly cold conditions, dampening the atmosphere early on as both sides slugged it out. Even the most unsympathetic fan would feel sorry for any neutral who'd decided to come and watch.

By the midway point of the first half, neither side had even registered a shot on target. The fans' frustrations grew with every misplaced pass. As the whistle blew for half-time, the teams slumped off to a chorus of boos. Based on this poor showing, FC Farce and Vickington Town looked shoo-ins for relegation.

In the second half, the game initially picked up where it left off. It was a drab, scrappy affair, with neither team able to take control. The groans from the stands only increased as the match wore on.

Then suddenly, around the hour mark the game sprang to life. Nelly Patterson picked up the ball from defence and began a mazy run down the wing. As he beat his first man, the home fans raised the noise decibels, urging their player to keep going.

'Go on, son!' Fred screamed on the touchline, waving him forward.

Nelly dribbled past another defender and managed to get his cross in. The wind took the ball perfectly towards Will Watkins, who rose above his man to connect cleanly with his head. The ball looped over the stranded goalkeeper and nestled into the roof of the net.

It was nearly a carbon copy of the goal that put them ahead in the cup game against Haverstone United. The home fans erupted with joy. Punching the air in delight, Fred quickly cooled, urging his players to keep their focus. Undeserved it might have been, the team had something to hold on to.

The game sparked an instant reaction from Vickington. The away team were equally desperate for points, throwing everything forward in search of an equaliser. FC Farce's back four coped admirably well, with no-nonsense centre back Clive Harrison thriving in the face of battle. Smithy pulled off a couple of vital saves, while at the other end, Percy Plumb missed a great opportunity to make it safe.

As the clock neared 90 minutes, Vickington Town seemed to be running out of ideas. As Fred frantically paced the touchline and barked instructions, it seemed FC Farce would hold on for a vital victory.

One minute into extra time, disaster struck. In a rare moment of panic, Clive put the ball out for a corner when he had the chance to boot it upfield. A mini stampede ensued as Vickington threw everybody including the goalie forward for the set piece, unsettling FC Farce's defence. The ball was played in, causing a mad scramble in the box, with the home fans screaming for the team to clear their lines.

Eventually, the ball fell to Vickington Town's tall striker, who met it with a looping header similar to Will Watkins' earlier goal. Smithy was nowhere — the ball eventually booted clear by Clive's centre back partner Tim Jenkins. But the ball had easily cleared the goal line.

Vickington Town's players wheeled away in jubilant celebration, while the home team looked crestfallen. On the sidelines, Fred slumped to his feet in despair, looking straight at the floor.

After bringing himself to glance painfully towards the pitch, a strange realisation hit Fred. Oddly, the referee hadn't blown his whistle. Had it stopped working? Fred thought back to the comical minute's silence incident. The ball was easily two yards over the line, he could see that from here.

Euphoria and disbelief washed over Fred as he realised that the referee was waving play on. He'd obviously been distracted by the melee from the box. Incredibly, neither of his linesmen had corrected his glaring error.

'Play on, boys!' screamed Fred, as his slumped players looked up in confusion. Having been swept up in a raucous celebration, the opposition players and management finally sensed something was amiss, but it took a few more moments for the injustice to hit home.

Once the penny dropped, everything went crazy. The opposition players' emotions completely shifted, surrounding the referee with fury and astonishment. It took several minutes to restore order. On the touchline, the opposition manager was apoplectic. He had to be separated from Fred after launching into a furious tirade. The FC Farce fans were loving it, loudly jeering their opponents as the complaints continued.

The unlucky striker took his remonstrations too far, the endless complaints resulting in a second yellow card. The delirious home fans waved as the player stormed down the tunnel in an angry puff of smoke, kicking a water bottle in frustration and narrowly missing Fred. FC Farce's manager continued to fan the flames, accusing him of doing it deliberately.

Once play finally resumed, FC Farce easily saw out the final few minutes to claim a priceless victory. The incensed Vickington Town players and bench continued to voice their grievances at the final whistle, with the opposition manager also receiving a red card for his troubles.

As FC Farce continued their celebrations, the travelling Vickington Town fans bizarrely found their voice in a loud chorus of cheers. The reason behind the strange shift in mood was initially unclear, but a glance towards the scoreboard revealed all.

Instead of 'FC Farce 1 Vickington Town 0,' it read, 'Cheats 1 Vickington Town 0 — fucking farce.'

A ripple of shock went around the ground as everyone witnessed the X-rated edit, but soon even the home fans started chuckling and seeing the funny side of it. On the touchline, Fred was absolutely furious, angrily gesturing at the opposition manager as he enthusiastically clapped the scoreboard.

Graham's face flushed red as he stared at the offending message. He shifted awkwardly, feeling the heat of the crowd's laughter. Meanwhile, the guy that controlled the scoreboard frantically tried to take it down. After several failed attempts and sweat pouring down his cheeks, the poor sod couldn't take it any longer.

'Ahhhhh!' He let out a loud wail, flinging his arms above his head in a state of hysteria before bolting full pelt out of the stadium. The chairman could only roll his eyes in dismay.

Typical, Graham thought to himself, shaking his head. *Just as we get some good luck, some nutter goes and tampers with the scoreboard.* The message continued to read loud and proud as the sniggering supporters eventually shuffled out of the stadium.

The unfortunate incident completely overshadowed the result, ensuring FC Farce hit the headlines for the wrong reasons again. As he sat reflecting on the latest catastrophe, Graham received a call from a familiar voice.

'Mr Farce, I'm thinking about adding your football club to our speed dial,' the football league official quipped, before ordering Graham to get to the bottom of the incident.

He needn't have worried. Graham was as outraged as the official, vowing to bring the culprit to justice. Graham hired an IT expert to investigate, who meticulously went through the digital files. The consultant examined the data for hours, expecting to find evidence of a hacker. Possibly a tech-savvy away fan. Graham restlessly sat on his hands as he awaited the verdict.

Gritting his teeth, the consultant eventually delivered the news. 'No sign of an intruder here,' he told Graham.

A cold shiver ran down Graham's spine. It meant it had to be an inside job.

Overnight, everyone at the club became a suspect, making for an uncomfortable environment. Calling an urgent staff meeting, the chairman urged the culprit to come forward.

Met with shifty glances and a deafening silence, Graham flinched. Familiar negative thoughts resurfaced, threatening to dampen his affection for the club all over again. Watching his staff slope off awkwardly, he hung his head low and wondered what to do next.

The next day, as he sat motionless in his office, there was a knock at Graham's door.

'Graham, have you got a sec?' the young club secretary asked.

Fred shrugged. 'Sure.'

Graham's interest piqued significantly when a tip-off was presented in his lap. With widening eyes, he examined a social media account belonging to stadium maintenance worker Johnny Marsden, revealing his allegiance to Vickington Town.

The profile was littered with bad language similar to that used on the tampered scoreboard, with a recent post even bemoaning the result against his employers. The colours drained from Graham's cheeks as he realised Johnny would have had access to the system that night.

Closing the laptop, his fists tightened as images of yesterday's staff meeting flashed through his mind. Johnny had stood there, bold as brash, not saying a word.

'He's got to be our man,' he later told Fred, after presenting him with the evidence.

Graham and Fred called Johnny into the office for a meeting. Fixing Johnny with a cold stare, they calmly explained what they'd found. The young lad was trembling, his eyes darting around the room looking for an escape route.

'Look, Johnny, it's up to you,' Graham said slowly, his eyes still firmly fixed on Johnny's. 'Either you admit what you've done, or we'll hand the evidence over to the police...'

'Alright, alright... it was me!' the young lad blurted out, visibly sinking into his chair. 'Please, don't call the police!'

That didn't take long, Graham thought, almost disappointed with how quickly Johnny had caved in.

'I didn't mean to cause the club any embarrassment,' Johnny sobbed, staring towards the floor.

Exchanging glances with Fred, the chairman sighed. For someone who'd managed to hack the club's scoreboard, this young lad clearly wasn't the brightest.

After letting him stew for a moment, Graham looked Johnny up and down. 'Since you've finally admitted what you did, I won't call the police. But I never want to see you set foot in this football club again, understood?'

Relief washing over him, Johnny nodded and darted out of the room.

⚽⚽⚽

With the bad apple disposed of, everyone could finally look forward to the Christmas party. On the big day, the marquee was spectacularly lit up and the dance floor was rocking, with the band keeping everyone entertained. More importantly, while the players and staff were having fun, Graham didn't see anybody taking their celebrations too far. He smiled at the merry but sensible scene, pleased that something was going well for a change.

Just as the party got in full swing, a sudden hailstorm battered the marquee, shaking it to its core. The temporary venue held firm, and most guests remained oblivious, but Graham felt a sense of unease. He'd failed to account for the unpredictable northern winter weather.

With growing anxiety, he cautiously examined the marquee, his concerns intensifying as the storm grew stronger. Ignoring his own advice, he nervously downed several glasses of wine to distract himself.

Fred noticed his chairman looked agitated. 'You alright, Graham?' he asked, seeing the chairman's glazed eyes. 'How much have you had?'

'I'm fine, thank you,' Graham slurred unconvincingly. 'Just enjoying myself.'

The manager rolled his eyes and walked away. 'Nice to see him taking it steady,' he muttered.

Graham took a moment to calm down. *Just relax,* he told himself. *The marquee will be fine.*

Unfortunately, Graham was wrong. Moments later, as the storm's fury escalated, the marquee groaned under the strain. Then with a deafening crack, the wind tore through the marquee like paper, ripping poles clean from the floor. In an instant, the party descended into chaos.

Plates of food spun through the air like frisbees, with one sausage roll smacking Graham square in the face. Drinks flew around like pigeons, drenching anyone unfortunate enough to be caught in their path. The dancefloor became an obstacle course of overturned chairs and people diving for cover.

Players and staff ducked and darted, some hiding under tables, others clinging to flailing tent walls in a desperate (but hopeless) attempt to hold things together. The band quickly bolted for safety — they hadn't signed up for an open-air venue.

It was a scene of mayhem all too familiar with FC Farce's season.

Panicking, the sozzled chairman made a snap decision to try and salvage everyone's experience. He sprinted onto the empty stage and grabbed the microphone. With the wind swirling furiously behind him, Graham held the mic to his lips, closed his eyes, and threw back his head.

'Silent niiiiiight! Holy...'

Half of the guests stopped to watch the chairman's impromptu solo in amazement, while half continued to dart around the destroyed venue. Graham's singing was easily drowned out by the wind and hail, but he ploughed on regardless. Commendably, some of the guests even started joining in, probably out of pity.

The bold act was more suited to his late father, Trevor — further proof of how stepping into the chairman's role had shaken Graham's once-reserved personality. At the end of the performance, Graham received a standing ovation.

'Thank you, thank you!' Graham shouted breathlessly, as the crowd continued to applaud him. 'Now, let's get out of here and head into town. I hope everyone's going to get as drunk as me!' This earned the loudest cheer of the night.

Graham dived into the adoring crowd, who carried him out of the shattered marquee to head for the bright lights of Henlon.

The next day, a groggy, sore-headed Graham winced as he opened his social media account. To his horror, some cheeky sod had uploaded the footage of his impromptu *X-Factor* audition —

making him quickly go viral. Cringing, Graham braced himself for tales of unsavoury incidents involving his players and staff. But to his relief, there was nothing bad to report. In fact, everyone had even chipped in to clean up the wrecked marquee, a testament to their growing togetherness.

In the final game before Christmas, the team's good behaviour was rewarded with a credible 1-1 draw away to promotion contenders Ruffleton Town. The result ensured FC Farce finished the year on a high, their form much improved after a poor start to the month.

'Go away and enjoy the Christmas break,' a beaming Fred told his players afterwards. 'You deserve it.'

With the calendar year drawing to a close, Graham was in a reflective mood. To put it mildly, his tenure at FC Farce had been a rollercoaster. He'd experienced more in a few months than most chairmen would experience in 10 years or more. There had been notable lows — the name change, multiple points deductions, invading sheep, and a destroyed marquee, just to name a few.

Only months ago, Graham had been a reluctant chairman, pulled into the football club by his father's legacy. Now, he felt more connected to this madcap team than he ever imagined. When FC Farce nearly pulled off a stunning upset at Haverstone United, he'd celebrated as wildly as anyone. He only wished his old man was around to see how the club had captured his heart.

Seeing in the new year with his family, he raised a glass to his father and looked forward to tackling the rest of the season. Whatever carnage it may throw at him!

CHAPTER 8

JANUARY – NEW YEAR BLUES

Fred's breath hung in the freezing January air as he watched his players warm up, tossing out soundbites of encouragement. As the new calendar year began, he dared to feel genuine hope. The team had lifted themselves from the foot of the table to the dizzy heights of second bottom. But with three teams set to be relegated, it would still be a huge task for FC Farce to stay up.

'What the hell was that all about?' the exasperated manager bellowed at his players just a few hours later.

After a second-half collapse, he'd just watched his side succumb to a 3-0 defeat away to Hexton United. The opponents were a typical run-of-the-mill mid-table side, solid but unremarkable. FC Farce's capitulation was deeply alarming.

As Fred demanded an explanation, the players stared at the floor in silence, deliberately avoiding his wild eyes. With no one willing to step up and be counted, his patience quickly wore thin.

'What have you got to say for yourselves?'

'Purrrp.' Somebody loudly farted. Not great timing.

Fred froze. 'Who the hell was that?' he growled, steam practically coming out of his ears.

The fart cut through the tense atmosphere like a knife, sending a gaggle of nervous sniggers around the room.

No one dared own up. With that, Fred stormed out of the dressing room in a huff, his previous goodwill and optimism shattered after another hopeless display.

'Sorry, lads,' Smithy whispered cautiously, glancing outside to make sure Fred wasn't still within earshot. 'Hard-boiled eggs at half-time probably wasn't the best idea.'

The following week, Graham sat alone at his desk, flipping through a stack of bills with growing concern. His mind kept circling back to the dwindling bank balance. Thanks to the farmer dispute, the money from the Haverstone United game was swallowed up as quickly as it came in. Costs were piling up, and Graham had never imagined just how much it would take to keep the club going.

The chairman's worries were interrupted by a knock at the door from his manager.

Fred cleared his throat. 'Graham, any chance we can bring in a few new players this January? After that rubbish on Saturday, it's clear we need reinforcements.'

Graham flinched at the untimely request. 'I'm sorry, it's just not going to be possible, Fred.'

Fred shifted uncomfortably, trying to hide his disappointment. 'I understand, Graham.'

Graham looked at his manager and blinked. He deserved a proper explanation.

'Look, I'll level with you,' he began, with a deep sigh. 'The club is barely staying afloat. As you know, attendances are down, and a few unexpected bills have put even more pressure on finances. Honestly, in a perfect world, we'd be trimming the squad, not adding to it.'

A wry smile tugged at Fred's lips. 'Well, at least I don't have to worry about losing anyone. No one would be interested in any of our lot!'

Graham chuckled in agreement, feeling some of the tension lift. 'Thanks for being so understanding, Fred. And try not to worry about things too much. I'm sure something will turn up soon.'

Just a few days later, Graham froze as he received a call from a panic-stricken Fred.

'Graham, the clubhouse is on fire! Get down here now!'

By the time Graham arrived, thick plumes of smoke billowed into the night sky, with firemen fighting to control the roaring flames.

'Bloody hell, how did this happen?' Graham stammered, staring at the destroyed building.

'It's the electrics,' a firefighter explained as he approached. 'Some dodgy wiring caught light, and the place went up like a matchstick.'

Graham exchanged a sombre look with Fred. Thankfully, no one was hurt, but the loss of clubhouse income would put an even greater strain on the club's finances.

'Say that again?' Graham spluttered the very next day, his grip tightening around the phone.

'I'm sorry, the policy expired on the clubhouse building last year,' the insurance agent replied grimly. 'It was never renewed.'

'That can't be possible!' Graham cried, frantically going back through his emails. 'I can't find any renewal notice. Where did you send it?'

'It was sent to Trevor Farce's email on the 30th of August last year.'

Graham's stomach dropped. That was just one week after his father's email redirect had expired. He'd missed it by a matter of days.

'I'm sorry, Mr Farce,' the agent continued softly. 'You will be solely responsible for the repair costs.' The line went dead.

The weight of the agent's words hit Graham like a sledgehammer. He slumped back in his chair, overwhelmed by the cruel timing. The fire alone was devastating — but this? It felt like a final nail in the coffin.

The club needed money fast. Desperately racking his brains, Graham eventually came up with a bold idea. A grand fundraiser. His plan was simple — host a fun-filled event at the club's grounds, bring the community together, and hopefully reignite the interest of fans who'd drifted away. It was a long shot, but Graham felt it could be just the boost they needed.

As he told Fred about the plans, the manager had an idea.

'Right, you lot,' Fred announced to his players with a mischievous grin. 'Since nobody owned up to that awful fart the other day, I've volunteered all of you to help out at the fundraiser. Everyone's got a job.'

A few audible groans murmured from within the group, with several players shooting glares in Smithy's direction. But the team nodded in resigned agreement.

⚽⚽⚽

'Fantastic!' Graham later exclaimed, leaning back in his office chair. 'I'll look forward to seeing you on the day.'

Hanging up the phone, he ticked off another name on his growing list. He'd managed to convince a team of local celebrities to take part in a friendly match against his side. Things seemed to be falling into place.

As the event drew closer, Graham grew increasingly hopeful that the day would be a success, seemingly forgetting all about the club's track record with such occasions. Catching a glimpse of the chairman's renewed optimism from behind her desk, Doris sighed.

'Sometimes desperation does funny things to you,' she muttered.

The big day arrived with beautiful sunny weather for late January. At the very least, there was no chance of a storm bringing a halt to proceedings.

The stadium was buzzing as the Henlon locals streamed in. The smell of fried onions and hot doughnuts filled the air, with an array of fun games and activities for the whole family. The atmosphere was warm and lively, with fans gleefully spotting local celebrities and mingling with players who happily posed for selfies.

Graham beamed with a mix of pride and relief. *Could this finally be the day things go smoothly?*

But true to form, things quickly unravelled. The bouncy castle was the centrepiece of the play area, but started deflating about an hour into the event. Gavin O'Donnell was tasked with supervising the inflatables and frantically tried to reinflate it, but the pump malfunctioned, resulting in a half-inflated, sagging mess resembling a deflated balloon.

Meanwhile, over-thinker Freddie Thompson was the auctioneer of the charity auction. He spent so long explaining the rules of the auction that by the time he got to the first item, most of the audience had wandered off in boredom. The few that hung around could hardly believe their luck as they were left to bid with no competition, securing items at bargain prices. Watching on, Graham glared at Freddie as he continued to pause and keenly examine the rules.

At least the friendly match itself showed early promise. Local celebrities, including the town's eccentric weatherman, lined up to face FC Farce. But disaster struck when captain Clive Harrison flattened a not-so-famous but undeniably handsome local actor with a crunching tackle. The poor man had to be carried off the pitch, much to the anger of many females in the crowd. The baying mob of admirers booed Clive's every touch, and he was substituted at half-time for his own safety.

In the second half, left back Barry McGraw unleashed a powerful shot that sailed high and wide, crashing straight into the food stand. Burgers and drinks flew through the air, drenching the crowd and sparking a minor frenzy as people scrambled to avoid the messy aftermath. It didn't match the havoc of the infamous sheep invasion, but it was enough to send several fans heading for the exits in disgust.

The rest of the game was a damp squib of a contest, with both sides keen to avoid any further injuries or damage. Like the earlier auction, many of the crowd shuffled off in boredom long before the full-time whistle.

The final straw came with the raffle draw. The sole prize, a signed FC Farce shirt, had actually drawn a decent number of ticket sales, a minor miracle given the day's fiascos. A thoroughly fed-up Graham reached into the raffle drum to pull the winning ticket — only to find it empty. Not a single ticket had been placed inside.

'Who was in charge of this?' Graham barked, holding up the drum.

'Old Bill,' someone mumbled from the back.

The chairman rolled his eyes and flung the shirt into the crowd, hoping that one of the kids at the front would get their hands on it. No such luck. A swarm of supporters furiously wrestled each other for the prized shirt, leaving several children in tears. Graham shook his head. The sorry scene summed up the day.

Worse still, as Graham later tallied up the bills for the damaged bouncy castle and food stand, he realised the club had barely broken even.

With the grand fundraiser falling flat, attentions temporarily turned to matters on the pitch. The next game was at home to Kibley Town, who'd comfortably beaten FC Farce 2-0 earlier in the season. Kibley were challenging for promotion and looked far superior opposition on paper — and on the pitch.

Much to the home fans' frustration, they scored early on and passed the FC Farce team to death. Incredibly, there was still only one goal in it moving into the final few minutes, even though Kibley had dominated proceedings. They had several chances but found Smithy in inspired form, despite the struggles of his teammates.

'C'mon, lads, keep your heads up!' Fred bellowed from the touchline, desperately hoping for something resembling a chance.

Unbelievably, FC Farce were handed a lifeline deep into injury time. Gavin O'Donnell picked up a loose ball in midfield and played it out to Nelly Patterson on the right, who'd hardly had a kick all game. He put his conserved energy to good use and took off down the wing like a madman, taking the previously untroubled Kibley Town defenders by surprise.

As he approached the corner flag, he feigned to cross, but skilfully bypassed the left back and headed inside towards the penalty area. In a moment of madness, the oncoming centre back panicked and clumsily brought Nelly down just as he moved into the box.

The home fans rose to their feet to scream for a penalty, but they needn't have worried. The ref had no hesitation in pointing to the spot. Disbelieving Kibley Town fans bemoaned their team's sloppiness, while FC Farce's supporters wildly celebrated their unexpected lifeline.

On the sidelines, Fred punched the air with his fist, delighted his prayers had been answered. Meanwhile, confusion suddenly reigned on the pitch.

'Who's taking it, boss?' Clive shouted towards the bench.

Fred ran his fingers through his hair. Will Watkins was the usual spot kick taker, but he'd already been hooked after a dreadful performance. The manager realised he hadn't considered who would step up in his absence.

Studying his players, Fred made a snap decision. 'Percy, it's yours,' he instructed, trying to hide his nagging doubts.

Percy nodded apprehensively. Fred watched as his player tentatively picked the ball up and jogged towards the penalty area. As Will's strike partner, Percy was the only obvious choice. But Fred couldn't shake off his feeling of dread.

As Percy put the ball down, the whole ground collectively held its breath. On the touchline, Fred's stomach churned. *Please score Percy*, he thought to himself, staring silently towards the heavens.

The final result was catastrophic. Percy took an almighty run up, but made the crucial mistake of changing his mind about where he was going to hit the ball. He hesitated, hesitated a bit more, before finally scuffing the ball so badly that it trickled towards the goal at a snail's pace. To everyone's disbelief, the goalkeeper simply had to bend down and pick it up to make the save.

The small section of Kibley Town fans celebrated with raucous laughter, deliriously taunting the home fans with an outpouring of chanting. Several of their players even fell over in hysterics. The rest of the ground looked on in stunned silence, while poor Percy sank to the turf, wishing the ground would swallow him up.

On the sidelines, Fred remained deathly silent, feeling like he'd been choked. As soon as the goalie booted the ball upfield, the referee blew his whistle. FC Farce had thrown away their get out of jail free card.

It was a cruel end to a strange encounter. Worse still, news came through to FC Farce's distraught bench that Vickington Town had picked up a surprise away win in their game. The team were dumped back to the foot of the table.

Unlike the last loss, where Fred had challenged his players for an explanation, the dressing room afterwards was completely numb. Everyone stared at the floor in deafening silence, with nobody able to bring themselves to offer any encouraging words.

Percy Plumb, with his head stooped low, hurriedly left the ground in his full kit before he'd even had a shower. Instead of anger, his gutted teammates actually felt sorry for him. It was quite simply the worst miss you could ever imagine.

The penalty debacle left the team's fragile confidence in tatters. Their final two games in January ended in consecutive 5-0 losses. It was déjà vu from their poor early December form, only this time worse.

After the second crushing 5-0 defeat, Fred trudged down the tunnel, shoulders weighed down with defeat. Angry chants from FC Farce supporters aimed firmly towards him pounded in his head. For the first time, doubts about his own future began circulating in his mind.

⚽⚽⚽

Despite the worrying run of form, Graham had no intention of making any changes where Fred was concerned. His mind was fully engrossed in the club's financial situation, which was growing more dire by the day. Costs continued to mount, and the balance sheet looked increasingly bleak. With no obvious solution in sight, Graham decided he had to bring in some outside investment.

The trouble was, bottom-of-the-table FC Farce wasn't exactly a tempting prospect for potential investors. As Graham scanned the club's worsening balance sheet, he thought back to the fans who packed the courtroom when Peter Oddsworth tried to get the club wound up. They'd fought tooth and nail to keep the club alive. Surely some of them would jump at the chance to get involved?

Graham took his idea public, inviting fans to share their views on a potential joint ownership model. The overwhelming social media response was completely at odds with the dwindling attendances, flooded with comments from hardcore supporters eager to get involved.

'About time the fans were given a proper voice!' one fan wrote. Graham scrolled through the messages, feeling a growing sense of cautious optimism. Encouraged by the enthusiasm, he arranged an open town hall meeting, hoping to turn the fans' excitement into something meaningful for FC Farce's future.

On the day of the event, the packed hall was buzzing with excitement as fans crammed into every available seat. Graham scanned the crowd, feeling a surge of pride, before stepping up to the podium. Clearing his throat, he launched into a frank overview of the club's finances, sparing no detail about just how badly FC Farce needed investment. The room went quiet, supporters exchanging worried glances as he laid out the situation.

But when he began explaining the potential benefits of a joint ownership model, the atmosphere changed for the better.

'You'll hold a tangible stake in this club,' Graham emphasised. 'Your voices will always be heard.' These promises brought the house down, the room erupting in applause.

His optimism growing, Graham opened the floor for suggestions. But things quickly began veering off course. The first hand shot up, and a man decked out in a full FC Farce kit enthusiastically rose to his feet.

'Fans need to have a say in team selection and subs!' he exclaimed. 'Just imagine — a real-time voting app, so we can vote on key decisions during matches!'

Nods of approval grew into rapturous applause, and Graham's smile wavered. He caught Fred's bewildered glance, who looked ready to bolt for the door.

Another supporter eagerly sprang up. 'We need to maximise non-matchday revenue,' the fan started, sounding like he might suggest something half-sensible.

'So, let's turn the stadium into a multi-purpose venue! We could put in a mini-golf course and a zip-line across the pitch!'

Graham visibly shuddered, the memory of the recent fundraising debacle flashing in his mind. He forced a nod, but felt a shiver as he imagined players ducking for cover from flying golf balls.

Just as the chairman was losing the will to live, an elderly fan leaned forward and raised a hand.

'We need to honour our old chairman properly — our late, great butcher Trevor...' he began, to which Graham nodded approvingly.

'How about erecting a giant pie outside of the stadium in his honour?'

The crowd clapped and cheered in agreement. Graham stared at the sea of nodding faces, beginning to question the sanity of his fanbase.

As the suggestions grew more ridiculous, Graham forced a smile and drew the meeting to a close. After the event, the club's management team was inundated with emails, letters, and social media posts containing other bizarre ideas.

Realising his plan was doomed to fail, Graham reluctantly abandoned the joint ownership idea. Upon reflection, he'd learnt that involving passionate, albeit well-meaning football supporters too closely was not always a good idea.

Although the episode brought an element of comedy to the situation, the reality remained deadly serious. FC Farce desperately needed some extra funds. Graham took the club's plea public once again, hoping to attract some genuine investment. He knew he was clutching at straws, and unsurprisingly, the chairman's act of desperation went unanswered.

The situation grew more precarious by the day. In the worst-case scenario — one Graham could barely bring himself to consider — the club could go out of business if it didn't secure additional investment soon. Graham was all in now, both financially and emotionally, and he vowed to do whatever it took to keep FC Farce afloat.

With their plight so dramatic, he even turned to the football league officials, appealing for financial support. Given how much trouble FC Farce had caused that season, it didn't take them long to say no (after they'd stopped laughing). Graham grew increasingly desperate and confided in his manager to get his take.

Fred appeared philosophical. 'Look, Graham, I know it seems bleak right now. I can't help much with the financial issues, but we both promised to do everything we can for this football club. We just have to keep going.' Graham nodded gratefully, relieved that his manager was still with him.

Fred had put on a brave face for his chairman, but privately he was extremely concerned. The team were in disarray. Based on their January form, they looked certain to go down. And then what? If the club's finances were as bad as Graham said they were, how long could the club realistically keep going? Especially with the drop in revenue after their inevitable relegation.

Later that evening, Graham tried to get an early night, but lay awake pondering the club's future. He stared at the ceiling, feeling the weight of his father's legacy pressing down harder with each passing minute.

All types of thoughts were circling around his head as he desperately tried to find solutions. As far as he was aware, the club had never faced any serious financial hardships when his father was at the helm. Maybe he wasn't up to being chairman after all?

Pull yourself together, man, he scolded himself. *You can get through this.*

As much as he tried, the reoccurring doubts refused to go away. Out of the blue, Graham was suddenly jolted from his thoughts by a phone call. It was an unknown number.

'Hello? Graham Farce here.'

There was a slight pause. 'Hi, Graham,' a voice eventually answered back.

The chairman recognised the mysterious voice, but couldn't work out who it was.

'Who is this, please?'

'Graham, I'm probably the last person you expected to hear from tonight. But it's Peter Oddsworth. I hear you're looking for an investor...'

CHAPTER 9

FEBRUARY — A DEAL WITH THE DEVIL

Graham held the phone away from his ear, jaw clenching as Peter Oddsworth's smooth voice echoed in his ears. This was the man who'd forced the club to change its name — the man who'd practically revelled in trying to dismantle his father's legacy. Just hearing his voice was enough to set Graham's pulse racing.

'You've got some nerve, Oddsworth,' he growled. 'After everything you've done to this football club? No chance.'

Peter Oddsworth chuckled lightly, undeterred by the venom in Graham's voice. 'Look,' he said calmly. 'Just hear me out. Five minutes, that's all I ask. I have a proposition that might... interest you.'

Graham's thumb hovered over the 'end call' button, but something held him back. On the other end of the line, Oddsworth launched into a polished pitch.

'I'll get to the point, Graham. I've watched FC Farce's season closely,' he began. 'Let's just say, I've really changed my perspective. I respect how your football club has handled everything it's come up against.'

Graham narrowed his eyes. 'Changed your perspective? After everything that's happened?'

'Yes, I can see why you'd feel that way,' Oddsworth continued, unfazed. 'But I've genuinely come to appreciate what the club brings to the community. I owe you an apology.'

Graham scoffed, his tone sharp. 'A bit late now, isn't it?'

Oddsworth chuckled softly. 'I want to make it up to you. The way I see it, you need an investor, one who has influence and resources.' He let the words settle, giving Graham a moment to absorb them.

'I'd be prepared to make a sizeable investment, enough to keep the club financially secure for years. New players, stadium upgrades, sponsorship opportunities — the lot.'

Graham swallowed, feeling his stomach twist. As Oddsworth shared more details, his proposal was almost too good to believe.

'And why exactly do you want to help us?'

'Simple,' Oddsworth replied matter-of-factly. 'The town of Henlon deserves a football club to be truly proud of. I believe I'm the one to help make that happen.'

Graham's mind raced. Oddsworth certainly had the money and the connections. But he also had the brass neck to suddenly say he was 'impressed' by the club. Something didn't feel right.

'I'm sorry, I just can't,' Graham finally stammered.

'Fine,' Peter Oddsworth replied smoothly, sensing Graham's hesitancy. 'You know where I am if you change your mind.'

Graham hung up, his hand shaking as he lowered the phone. As he lay awake in bed that night, Oddsworth's words continued to gnaw away at him.

On one hand, the proposal was everything the club needed. A cash injection, resources to finally get FC Farce on its feet, and a shrewd partner who knew how to navigate local businesses. Peter Oddsworth had a reputation for getting things done, and Graham couldn't deny that the club's future was looking bleaker by the day.

But the downside was obvious. He'd be inviting a man into the heart of the club who'd once tried to block his father from buying it in the first place. Could he really trust Peter Oddsworth?

The following morning, Graham's head was still spinning. He tentatively reached for his phone and dialled a number.

'Hello?'

Graham hesitated, his grip tightening on the phone, but then he thought of the club's empty bank account. 'OK, I'll hear you out,' he muttered, barely containing his reluctance. 'But not anywhere local; I'll find us somewhere quiet to meet.'

'Excellent!' Oddsworth beamed triumphantly, delighted that

his confidence hadn't been misplaced. 'See you then.'

The following week, Graham's apprehension grew as he approached the small, out-of-town Italian restaurant where they'd agreed to meet. Inside, Oddsworth was already waiting in a quiet corner, unmistakable in his trademark blue suit. He greeted Graham with a confident nod, and after a brief exchange of tense pleasantries, the two men settled into their seats. The restaurant was virtually empty, creating a quiet backdrop to the meeting.

Oddsworth wasted no time. 'Let's cut to the chase, shall we?' he said, leaning forward. 'I see this club as more than just an investment opportunity. It's a community asset, and with the right approach, we could elevate it beyond even your father's dreams.'

Graham nodded, though unease prickled at the back of his mind. Oddsworth repeated his grand plans for the club, everything FC Farce needed to thrive. And yet, as he spoke, Graham couldn't shake the feeling of a trap being laid.

'I'll admit, it all sounds great,' Graham tentatively conceded. 'But why do you suddenly want to help us?'

'Look,' Oddsworth began, a wry smile forming on his lips. 'I'm a businessman. I wouldn't be interested if I didn't think I'd eventually see some kind of return on my investment. But I also want what's best for the club and the community. You'll have to trust me on that one.'

As the conversation progressed into the final details, Graham found himself nodding along. Oddsworth's proposals were certainly plausible. But it was the way he talked about FC Farce as being an investment opportunity that raised red flags.

'I'll think about everything you've said,' Graham promised after they'd finished their lunch. 'I'll be in touch.' Oddsworth held out his hand, and after a brief moment of hesitation, Graham shook it.

⚽⚽⚽

The following morning, as Graham reached for the morning newspaper, his tired eyes jolted wide open at the bold, damning headline:

'FC Farce Chairman Dines With The Devil!'

A shiver ran down his spine. There it was in black and white — a photo of him shaking Oddsworth's hand at yesterday's lunch. A reporter must have found out about the meeting, landing the perfect scoop for the local front pages. His pulse racing, Graham grabbed his phone and called Fred in a state of panic.

'The article's all wrong!' he spluttered. 'They're making it sound like a done deal. I haven't agreed to anything yet!'

Fred listened intently, his voice sympathetic but frank. 'Graham, I wish you'd told me about the meeting. I know you had good intentions, but the fans won't see it that way.'

That was an understatement. FC Farce's fans were outraged, flooding social media with seething posts. How could Graham even consider letting a man like Oddsworth into their beloved club?

The anger in their words hit Graham like a punch to the gut. He wanted what was best for the club, and it looked like he had two choices: ignore the financial situation and risk FC Farce's future, or do a deal with Oddsworth and risk ruining his relationship with the fans. Much like when he'd been thrust into taking over the club after his father's death, Graham found himself caught between a rock and a hard place.

Amidst the drama, the team's first game in February was a crucial away match against old foes Vickington Town. Since December's controversial scoreboard-gate clash, which FC Farce won thanks to a clear equaliser being disallowed, Vickington had gone on a decent run and stood just one point away from safety. Meanwhile, FC Farce had taken their place at the bottom, and in serious danger of being cut adrift.

The home side looked fired up, determined to get revenge for December's injustice. Even their scruffy mascot, Vicky the Dog, looked pumped up for the occasion, literally barking at the startled FC Farce players and hopping around on all fours. FC Farce's away supporters turned up in good numbers for the fixture, ensuring a red-hot atmosphere in the ground.

In light of the Peter Oddsworth saga, some fans booed as Graham climbed the steps to the director's box. He paused, glancing toward the familiar faces in the away stands, each jeer feeling like a jab. Swallowing his hurt, Graham forced a polite nod before sinking into his seat and turning his focus towards the match. Meanwhile, Fred urged his side to keep calm and not be distracted by the noise.

The game kicked off with both teams looking jittery, but it was clear that FC Farce were the more aggressive side. They pressed forward with intent, their forwards snapping at the heels of Vickington's defenders, forcing them into a series of desperate clearances. A fired-up Fred encouraged his side to move the ball wide as much as possible, making use of Nelly Patterson's pace down the right wing.

And it was Nelly who created the first real chance of the game. In the 23rd minute, he burst past his marker and whipped in a low cross. Skipper Clive Harrison rarely ventured past the halfway line, but after a rush of blood to the head, charged forward to slam home the opener.

1-0 to FC Farce, and delirious celebrations in the away end. The Vickington Town fans looked perplexed. Were they facing their bogey team?

As the first half wore on, FC Farce managed to hold their lead, but it was clear that Vickington Town weren't going to roll over easily. They gradually asserted themselves, their midfield starting to control the tempo of the game. But FC Farce held on to their slender lead, Smithy coming to their rescue on several occasions.

Meanwhile, Vickington's mascot Vicky the Dog had taken a particular interest in winding up FC Farce's left back Barry McGraw. The scruffy dog barked at Barry every time he got the ball, mimicking his movements and exaggerating every mistake. It seemed harmless enough, but Barry was growing visibly tired of being singled out.

'Lino!' Barry yelled, pointing accusingly at Vicky the Dog. 'Have a word, will you!'

The linesman shrugged. He clearly wasn't overly interested in dealing with an overexcited mascot. Eventually, half-time came with FC Farce still leading 1-0.

'Excellent, lads!' Fred beamed at the interval. 'Keep your focus and discipline, and we'll do this lot again!'

After the interval, Vickington Town turned the screw, dominating possession and launching wave after wave of attack. Fred paced the touchline, shouting instructions and urging his players to dig deep.

FC Farce were just 15 minutes from victory, but the pressure finally told. A speculative cross wasn't dealt with properly, and the ball fell kindly for Vickington's striker, who slammed it into the roof of the net from close range. 1-1.

Vicky the Dog, having been more reserved in the second half, suddenly sprang back to life. He bounded over to the touchline where Barry McGraw stood, who was deeply frustrated to have conceded so cheaply. The mascot began an over-the-top celebration, loudly barking and wildly shaking his paws at FC Farce's furious left back.

'Shut up!' Barry shouted at the scruffy mascot, anger bubbling inside him.

Vicky the Dog ignored the warning, pointing dramatically at Barry, as if to say, 'This is on you, mate!' The home fans laughed and joined in with the lairy mascot's taunts.

In a flash, Barry McGraw snapped. He lunged at Vicky the Dog and caught him with a clean punch on his oversized face. The mascot fought straight back, pouncing on Barry and trading blows as they rolled around on the floor. Fans gasped in amazement as they witnessed the astonishing scenes.

On the sidelines, Fred was incredulous. 'What the bloody hell is going on over there!' he cried, as the surreal punch-up continued.

Players from both sides rushed over to separate them. But the sight of a grown man wrestling with a giant dog proved too much for some, who ended up joining in the melee. What began as a two-man scuffle quickly escalated into a full-blown brawl, with bodies flying everywhere from both sides.

Once order was finally restored, the dumbfounded referee was left to make sense of it all. Following a brief and rather animated discussion with his assistants, he pulled out his red card and sent off Barry McGraw. The player walked off the pitch to a chorus of 'Cheerio!' from the home fans, while Fred fixed him with a hostile glare. Bizarrely, the mascot was also sent off, not that it made much difference to events on the pitch.

With the man advantage, Vickington Town surged forward. Just five minutes later, their right winger broke down the exposed left-hand side, delivering a pinpoint cross that was headed powerfully into the bottom corner. 2-1 to Vickington Town, and the home fans were in raptures. On the sidelines, Fred sank to the floor in dismay.

The final whistle blew moments later. Another painful loss for FC Farce. Provoked or not, Barry McGraw's sending off had cost them dearly. The home team celebrated wildly, with tempers threatening to spill over again as the players went down the tunnel.

Back in the safety of the dressing room, it was clear who Fred blamed for the defeat. 'What the hell was all that about?' Fred screamed at Barry McGraw.

The player sat with his shoulders slumped, staring at the floor. 'It was the mascot, boss,' he mumbled. 'He started it.'

'The mascot started it!' Fred growled. 'Do you have any idea how ridiculous that sounds?'

Turning his back on the player, he delivered his brutal verdict. 'You've cost us today, lad.'

Barry sank in his seat, while his teammates exchanged subtle glances. The manager's words were harsh, but he was clearly feeling the pressure.

'So, what did you make of the Barry McGraw incident?' a keen reporter later asked Fred in his post-match interview.

Clearing his throat, Fred's view completely changed for the cameras. 'I didn't really see what happened,' he lied. 'But from what I've been told, their idiot mascot instigated the whole thing by provoking Barry McGraw. I'm sure the football league will show leniency.' Of course, the plea went unnoticed, with a three-match ban duly following.

⚽⚽⚽

The manager wasn't the only one feeling the pressure. Back in his office, Graham continued to grapple with the Peter Oddsworth dilemma. The council leader had given him a week's deadline to decide, or any potential deal would be off.

Out of the blue, the phone rang. It was Brian Luxton, Graham's solicitor. The chairman twitched. Something told him it wasn't going to be good. Was it something to do with the football club? He wondered if Peter Oddsworth had already put the wheels in motion. Eventually, Graham took the call.

'Hi, Brian,' he began nervously. 'How can I help?'

'Hi, Graham,' Brian replied brightly. 'I've got some news that might interest you…'

Brian continued, his voice steady but tinged with anticipation. 'Graham, several years ago, your father set up a secret trust fund to protect the club's future,' he explained. 'It's only just come to light, but it's substantial.'

He deliberately coughed before revealing the exact amount. Graham's jaw dropped as he heard the figure. The trust fund easily dwarfed Oddsworth's offer, with more than enough to secure the club for many years.

As the scale of the news hit home, Graham broke into a wide grin.

'I'm just sorry we've only just discovered it,' Brian said with a chuckle.

'Are you kidding?' cried Graham, his heart pounding with excitement. 'This is the best news I could ever have hoped for! Thank you so much, Brian.'

'No problem! If you like, I'll send you a copy of the details now so you can see it for yourself. Look out for an email in the next few minutes.'

Hanging up, Graham punched the air in delight, the euphoria flooding through him. It was as if the weight of the world had been lifted from his shoulders. It had to be fate — his father would never have wanted him to make a deal with Oddsworth. And now, thanks to the newly discovered trust fund, he wouldn't have to. Relieved and energised, Graham eagerly refreshed his emails in anticipation of Brian's message.

Moments later, an email came through. But it wasn't from Brian. Confused, Graham clicked on it and opened the attachment. As he skimmed the document, his eyes widened. He was speechless for the second time in just a few minutes. His teeth clenched as he absorbed the contents, each line exposing the depths of betrayal in black and white.

As Graham processed the shocking development, another notification appeared on his screen: 'This email has been recalled by the sender.' The message disappeared, and seconds later Graham's phone rang.

It was Oddsworth. His tone was unusually sheepish. 'Graham, I think I may have accidentally sent you something. You didn't, um, happen to see an email from me just now?'

Graham's demeanour completely shifted. 'An email?' he replied calmly. 'No, I'm not at my desk at the moment. Why? Was it important?'

Oddsworth attempted to hide his relief. 'Oh, no, nothing important at all. No need to worry. It was for another client, so I just wanted to make sure you hadn't seen it.'

Graham continued to keep his composure. 'No problem at all. Actually, I'm glad you phoned Peter, I was just about to give you a call. I've been thinking about your offer, and I think it's exactly what the club needs. I'd like to accept your proposal.'

For a moment there was silence. Now, Oddsworth's voice was laced with excitement. 'Really? That's wonderful news!'

'Yes — I'm glad we could put the past behind us. For the club's sake,' Graham replied coolly. 'Tell you what, why don't we announce it at a press conference on Friday? Make it all official?'

'Sounds great!' Oddsworth cooed, delighted to have finally won over his old rival. 'I'll leave you to get that sorted. Thanks, Graham, I'm looking forward to working with you.'

Graham put the phone down. 'I bet you are, Peter,' he said with a smirk. 'I bet you are.' As he pieced together his next move, another email came through. It was Brian Luxton, confirming the trust fund's legitimacy.

With Oddsworth's cooperation, the wheels were quickly put in motion for Friday's press conference. Rumours circulated that the council leader would be acquiring a sizeable stake in the club, and the fans once again went into meltdown. Graham's office was inundated with calls from angry supporters voicing their grievances.

'Wait and see,' the chairman said throughout, keeping his cool amidst the outrage. 'All will be revealed.' He was excited and nervous for Friday in equal measure.

When the big day arrived, the press conference was filled with reporters, league officials, and fans eager to hear the big announcement. At the front, Graham took his seat next to a smug Peter Oddsworth. The council leader clearly revelled in the attention, practically bursting at the seams to deliver the news.

As the cameras flashed, Graham gestured for Oddsworth to speak first. Gritting his teeth, he listened to the council leader waffle on for several minutes, painting himself as the hero of Henlon.

'And, so,' Oddsworth finally announced, glancing with a thin smile towards Graham. 'It gives me great pleasure to announce that I will be making a substantial investment in FC Farce, in return for a sizeable stake in the football club.'

The room's atmosphere turned electric, an audible hiss of fury rising from the fans. The announcement came as no surprise, but it was sickening to hear it from the horse's mouth. As the booing grew louder, Oddsworth flashed a huge grin at the restless crowd, revelling in the moment.

However, the biggest twist was yet to come.

A reporter stood up, directing his question to Graham. 'Mr Farce, after all that's happened, how do you feel about allowing Mr Oddsworth to invest in the club?'

Oddsworth leaned forward eagerly, his smile widening as he anticipated Graham's glowing response. Graham held his gaze steady, masking his nerves with a carefully controlled expression.

'I'm sorry,' Graham began slowly, his voice calm. 'But I have absolutely no idea what this man is talking about.'

Gasps rippled throughout the room. Oddsworth's confident grin faltered, the reporters around him sensing that this press conference was about to take an unexpected turn.

The chairman continued confidently. 'Quite frankly, I wouldn't let this man anywhere near FC Farce. I wouldn't take any notice of him.' The colour drained from Oddsworth's cheeks.

Graham paused deliberately, letting the anticipation hang in the air. 'Actually, I called this press conference to let Mr Oddsworth explain why, as this town's council leader, he wants to demolish our stadium and replace it with a housing estate.'

After a split-second moment of stunned silence, the room exploded. Fans surged to their feet, hurling angry accusations at Oddsworth, as reporters scrambled forward to bombard him with questions. Eventually, after several minutes of chaos, the flustered council leader raised his hands, desperately trying to calm the uproar.

'These accusations are absurd,' he spluttered. 'Quite frankly, I'm appalled by Graham's behaviour. I've submitted a generous proposal that he's verbally accepted, and I was under the impression that we were here today to share the news. I can only apologise that this man is clearly wasting everyone's time.'

Graham looked his rival square in the eye, before delivering the killer blow. 'Explain this, then!' he boomed, brandishing a copy of the architect's drawings. He'd managed to save a copy that Oddsworth had mistakenly sent him just before he recalled the email. The game was up.

Oddsworth's face went ghostly pale. Graham handed copies

of the documents to the reporters, who quickly scanned the shocking plans. The anger in the room went up a notch as the damning evidence stood clear in black and white.

Realising he was cornered, Oddsworth stammered out a feeble, 'No comment!' before bolting from the room before he was lynched. His abrupt exit echoed the name-changing tribunal at the start of the season. Only this time, Graham had the upper hand.

After briefly pausing to savour the sweet moment, Graham stood to address the room for a final time.

'One last thing, folks. We've recently discovered a trust fund that my late father, Trevor, left for the club. With it, our finances are secure.' He paused, his face breaking out into a huge smile. 'FC Farce won't be needing any outside help.'

Within the blink of an eye, the crowd erupted in a roar that shook the walls. Chants of 'Graham!' echoed through the room. Graham's chest tightened with pride, a lump forming in his throat. As he soaked in the fans' cheers, he knew he'd done his father proud. The press conference stunt had pushed him to his limits, but it had paid off spectacularly.

As for Oddsworth, the fallout from the press conference was swift and brutal. Stung by the public outcry, the authorities immediately launched investigations into his other business dealings. More shady practices came to light, leading to charges of corruption and fraud. His reputation, and his legacy, lay in ruins.

In a poetic twist of fate, Oddsworth's attempt to exploit FC Farce ultimately caused his own downfall.

CHAPTER 10

MARCH – UNFORTUNATE RESIGNATIONS

With the club's financial troubles behind them, Graham was elated, but Fred felt the season weighing on him more than ever. FC Farce were still bottom of the league, and while Graham was buoyed by his recent victory over Oddsworth, the battle on the pitch looked as bleak as ever. Fred put on a brave face for the players, but with each game, the situation felt increasingly hopeless.

At the end of the day, the team's form was abysmal, and Fred couldn't see where their next win would come from. In fact, the most passion he'd seen from anyone on the pitch recently was when Barry McGraw had a fight with the opposition mascot. On the plus side, at least there was enough money in the kitty to finally strengthen the squad. Too bad the bloody transfer window was closed!

FC Farce's first game in March ended in a desperate 3-0 defeat away to Retton United. The opposition barely broke sweat, but were still fitter and sharper in every department. Buoyed by the recent press conference, the travelling fans had given the team a rousing reception, but soon grew frustrated at the hapless showing.

After the final whistle, Fred's patience snapped. He avoided the dressing room, ignored waiting reporters, and left the stadium without a word to anyone. Watching his manager speed away from the stadium, Graham's mind drifted back to their conversation before the infamous fans' forum. They'd promised to stick together whatever they faced that season. The chairman couldn't help feeling disappointed in the abrupt exit.

Fred's own thoughts returned to that conversation. He'd

promised to give everything to keep the team in the division, but what did he have to work with? By Combinations Premier League standards, his players were woeful, and he was growing tired of their lacklustre performances. Not to mention the chaos that had followed the club everywhere that season.

Following a 2-0 home defeat to Brackington Town and yet another chorus of boos, Fred found himself seriously questioning his position. He'd been determined to see out the season, but what was the point of sticking around just to suffer an inevitable relegation?

Having spent so many years in the game, Fred could see the writing on the wall. The team would go down, and Graham would say something like, 'Thanks for everything, but it's time for a new direction.' Then the new manager would be handed a big transfer kitty, before being lauded as a hero for getting them back up.

In reality, the depressing picture Fred had painted in his head couldn't have been further from the truth. While the Brackington game had been another dismal showing, the chairman had no intention of sacking Fred — even if the club went down. He'd seen the mess Fred had been handed and respected how he'd held things together. The trust fund had completely turned around the club's finances, and Graham was looking forward to a brighter future with Fred at the helm.

But Fred couldn't see past the here and now, and his frustration had him teetering on the edge. He'd just watched his team lose for the umpteenth time, with Brackington Town's bench even joining in the ridicule. Most of the laughs were aimed at the unfortunate keeper Smithy, who'd somehow let Brackington's first goal dribble through his legs before face-planting in the mud.

Angry with himself, Smithy kicked the goalpost in frustration and injured his foot, forcing Fred to replace him with Shorty, their five-foot backup keeper. Predictably, Brackington chipped in two further efforts hopelessly out of reach of his despairing dives, sending the opposition bench into fits of laughter. Fred could barely stand to watch.

That night, Fred tossed and turned, thoughts tumbling around in his head. He'd promised Graham he'd see things through, but what was the point of hanging around to be relegated and sacked? The more he thought about it, the clearer it seemed. If he resigned now, a new manager could step in and assess the squad ahead of the inevitable summer clear-out. In his mind, stepping down made sense for all parties.

By morning, his mind was made up. With a heavy heart, he wrote an official letter of resignation before jumping in his car and driving to Graham's office. As he made his way there, doubts crept in, but he convinced himself it was the right thing to do.

After a brief moment's hesitation, Fred took a deep breath and knocked on the door. Graham greeted him with a warm smile, looking a bit puzzled.

'Hi, Fred,' Graham said, raising his eyebrow. 'What brings you here?'

Fred swallowed, glancing at the floor. 'Um, I need to speak to you about something,' he mumbled. 'Have you got a few minutes?'

'Sure!' Graham replied brightly, clearly unaware of anything amiss. 'Actually, there's something I've been meaning to discuss with you. Do you mind if I go first?'

This knocked Fred off his stride. 'Uh... okay. Go ahead.'

Graham looked his manager in the eyes. 'First, I just want to say a huge thank you for everything you've done this season,' he began. 'It's been an incredibly tough year, and you've had an enormous amount to contend with. Your efforts are greatly appreciated.'

Fred shifted uncomfortably, his mind spiralling. It sounded like his chairman was leading up to something. Was he planning to sack him anyway?

'Despite your best efforts, we both know there's a good chance FC Farce will be relegated this season,' Graham continued, with a slight frown.

Here we go, Fred thought, bracing himself for the inevitable. He could feel his own resignation letter burning a hole in his back pocket. Maybe he should get in there first...

'But I think you've done a remarkable job with the resources at your disposal. And now, with our financial troubles behind us, I'd like to offer you an improved contract as FC Farce's manager.' Graham grinned. 'And you'll have a significantly increased budget for new signings next season — no matter what league we're in.'

Fred stared, unable to hide his shock. 'A new contract?'

Graham nodded. 'You deserve it, Fred. Your loyalty this season has been unquestionable.'

Fred forced a shaky smile. Imagine if Graham knew what he had in his back pocket...

'Wow... I really don't know what to say. Thank you, Graham. I'm genuinely over the moon!'

'Don't mention it,' Graham replied with a wink. 'You've earned it.'

After a brief pause, Graham's expression shifted. 'Oh, was there something else you wanted to talk about?'

Fred's mind raced. 'Oh, uh, no — nothing important. Just that Smithy's injury isn't serious. He'll be back for Saturday.'

'Great!' Graham said with a chuckle. 'Shorty tried his best, but let's face it, he's hardly a giant between the sticks.'

'True enough,' Fred laughed, instantly relaxing. 'Thanks again, Graham. Rest assured; I'll do everything I can to keep us up.'

The shift in his fortune left Fred stunned. Graham had backed him all along, and Fred felt foolish for doubting him. His resolve hardened — if FC Farce were going down, they'd go down fighting. With a spring in his step, he headed home, pouring himself a large glass of red to celebrate his new contract.

Eventually dozing off on the sofa, Fred was suddenly woken a few hours later by a phone call. It was his chairman.

'Hi, Graham,' Fred muttered, still groggy with sleep. 'Everything okay?'

Graham's tone was suddenly cold. 'Well, I thought it was,' he replied. 'Fred, I was extremely disappointed to find out about your news. But, reluctantly, I'm phoning to accept your resignation.'

Fred's heart stopped. He patted his back pocket, feeling nothing but the empty fabric. The note was gone. Panic shot through him, and he struggled to find his voice. 'What... how did you...'

'I was handed your resignation note,' Graham interrupted. 'I must say, I'm disappointed you didn't discuss it with me first, choosing to put it in writing...'

Fred froze, his mind racing. The note must have slipped from his pocket and been discovered. He wanted to tell Graham it was all a mistake, to explain he never intended to hand in his notice. But the words stuck in his throat.

'I... I'm sorry, Graham,' he mumbled finally, then quickly ended the call. Unbelievably, he'd managed to accidentally resign from his own job.

A mess of emotions surged through him as he slumped back onto the sofa. He'd let his own frustrations cloud his judgement, throwing away the job he now realised he'd loved all along.

In a cruelly ironic twist, Fred later learnt that of all people, it was Old Bill the kit man who'd fatefully discovered the note. It was probably the first time he'd ever been observant in his life!

The next morning, the bombshell headline hit the back pages: 'Fred F's Off!' Fans flooded local radio stations, expressing anger and disbelief at yet another twist in FC Farce's turbulent season.

By the afternoon, Fred had finally pulled himself together. He was going to speak with Graham and explain it had all been a mistake. He'd beg for his job back if he had to.

Fiercely determined, Fred jumped into his car and headed for the football club. He strode through the main entrance, ignoring the receptionist's protests of 'You can't go in there!' and barged straight into the chairman's office. He immediately regretted his decision.

Two men glared back at him. Graham looked up, eyebrows raised in anger, while a smartly dressed man next to him was mid-presentation. Fred's stomach dropped as he realised he'd just gate-crashed an interview for his own job.

'What on earth do you think you're doing?' Graham boomed.

'You handed in your resignation yesterday, remember? You can't just burst in here while I'm interviewing your replacement!'

The shock deflated Fred completely. 'Uh... sorry, Graham,' he mumbled, barely able to look his chairman in the eye. 'I didn't realise. I just came to collect some of my things. To say goodbye.'

'I see,' Graham said, his expression hardening. 'Well, you've said goodbye now. Off you go then.'

Head stooped low, Fred turned and left the office. He'd never felt so foolish. His former chairman had clearly moved on, and he only had himself to blame for letting his job slip through his fingers.

No sooner had Fred left the building, rumours quickly began circulating that Poldon Borough's manager, Keith Baxter, was the frontrunner for the position. Ironically, he currently managed one of the few teams that FC Farce had actually beaten that season. Fred was distraught. Once feeling disillusioned by the club's chaos, he longed for its topsy-turvy environment. He couldn't see himself anywhere else.

⚽⚽⚽

With no new manager in place yet, Coach Steve took charge of FC Farce's final game in March. The team were at home to Dryden Town, and a strange atmosphere hung in the air as the players entered the pitch. Steve, more suited to one-on-one training drills, was visibly out of his depth in this environment.

Confused players darted around like headless chickens, their movements disjointed and frantic as they looked to the sidelines for anything resembling guidance from their temporary leader. Lacking inspiration, they limped through 90 painful minutes, suffering another routine 3-0 defeat that nudged FC Farce even closer to relegation.

The shambolic showing only soured Graham's mood further. He'd stayed loyal to Fred, even offering him an improved contract. But clearly, that hadn't been enough. Graham felt a mix of betrayal and disappointment. For all he knew, Fred already had another opportunity lined up. As he'd quickly learnt, there was no such thing as loyalty in football. So, Graham knew he had to put the old manager behind him and move on.

Despite his determination to get the matter resolved, Graham couldn't shake his doubts about Keith Baxter. There was something theatrical, even highly strung about him. Still, Keith's managerial record was half-decent, and there hadn't exactly been a flood of applications.

After a few days of reflection, Graham decided to make the offer. Keith accepted enthusiastically, launching immediately into an ambitious list of plans for FC Farce. Impressed by his new manager's energy, Graham pushed aside his lingering hesitations and prepared for another press conference — hopefully a less eventful one than when he outed Oddsworth.

Meanwhile, Fred continued to wallow in misery about his accidental departure. On the day of the announcement, Fred was drowning his sorrows at The Bull Arms, the same spot where he and Graham had once won over the supporters during the infamous fans' forum. The memory of Graham tumbling off the stage after his slurred, incoherent speech brought a fleeting smile. Back then, they'd been a team, united with their fans. He craved a return of those days.

Any hopes of ignoring the press conference were dashed when the pub's telly switched to the live broadcast. As he took a swig, Fred glanced reluctantly at the screen, where reporters and fans packed the room around Graham. Then the announcement confirmed the rumours: Keith Baxter appointed as FC Farce manager.

'Him?' Fred blurted out, half-cut. 'My cat could do a better job.'

As the event got underway, he watched flamboyantly dressed Keith swagger to the podium and launch into his opening remarks. Keith rattled off strange, boastful promises about the team's future, his comments so exaggerated that it was hard to tell if he was genuinely being serious. Even though he'd had more than a few drinks, Fred could sense his ex-chairman's unease, watching Graham's forced smile grow tighter with each bizarre comment.

Fred continued watching with interest, shaking his head

as Keith fired off one outlandish statement after another. As awkward glances passed through the crowd, the chairman's face told its own story. Fred could almost see the wheels spinning in his mind, trying to convince himself that this was the right choice.

With a mix of alcohol and adrenaline rushing through him, Fred decided it wasn't too late. The dishevelled ex-manager sprinted out of the pub and headed straight for the live press conference — taking place just around the corner. He had nothing to lose, so he was going to tell his chairman how he really felt once and for all.

Stumbling slightly, Fred bolted towards the venue, pushing past a few surprised onlookers. To his amazement, no security stopped him as he headed straight for the front of the room. He barely registered the astonished faces around him as he burst into the press conference, his confidence evaporating only when Graham looked at him with exasperation.

'Fred!' Graham cried, shaking his head. 'What on earth are you doing, man? We're here to announce your replacement. You handed in your notice, remember?'

Fred took a deep breath, swallowing his nerves. 'Look, Graham, that was a mistake. I didn't mean to resign. I'll do whatever it takes to get my job back. Please.' He looked into his chairman's eyes, his voice thick with sincerity.

Stunned reporters exchanged brief glances, ready to pounce on this latest twist. Graham stared towards Fred, too amazed to respond. *Only at FC Farce*, he thought, *could something like this happen*. Graham's mind raced at a hundred miles an hour as he grappled with what to do next. The room fell silent, keenly anticipating his next move.

Keith Baxter got there first, reacting hysterically to the turn of events.

'Are you insane?' he shrieked, angrily pointing towards Fred. 'I'm the manager now! I'll have you arrested for trespassing! Security? Security!' He spluttered out the last words with a wild sweep of his arms, frantically looking around for help that didn't arrive. His embarrassing theatrics only seemed to amuse the gathered press, a few of whom chuckled at his expense.

'Graham!' Keith cried, continuing to wave his arms. 'Tell this idiot to leave at once!'

Graham hesitated, caught between his doubts over Keith and Fred's impromptu appeal. He really didn't want to make a decision of this magnitude on the spot.

Outraged not to receive instant backing from his new chairman, Keith took the dilemma out of his hands.

'Well then!' Keith huffed, placing his hands on his hips. 'You've made your feelings perfectly clear. You clearly want that imbecile over me!' With that, Keith spun on his heel and stormed out of the press conference, muttering obscenities as he slammed the door behind him.

The press room erupted in laughter. For the second time in a month, an FC Farce press conference had descended into complete chaos. Sighing deeply, Graham glanced at Fred, who was still a bit dazed from his impromptu decision.

He looked his old manager square in the eye. 'Fred,' he began seriously. 'Are you 100% committed to this football club?'

Fred nodded with conviction. 'Yes, Graham. I give you my word. I want this job more than anything.'

Graham's face softened. 'Well then,' he shrugged, turning to the press with a grin. 'I guess I need to announce the sudden resignation of Keith Baxter. We thank him for all his hard work and wish him the very best for the future.' The assembled fans and reporters sniggered.

'And now,' Graham continued, his eyes twinkling, 'I'm pleased to announce the reappointment of Fred Cotton, making him our third manager of the season!'

The room broke out in hysterics for the final time. Fred shook his head in disbelief, overcome with gratitude and joy. Hugging Graham, he felt an immense relief. Somehow, his crazy decision to gatecrash the press conference had worked. He'd gotten his job back.

And for Graham, it felt like yet another weight had been lifted. He and Fred finally stood side by side once more, ready to face the remainder of this unpredictable season together.

CHAPTER 11

APRIL – TACTICAL PROTEST

Fred's unexpected comeback sent a wave of excitement through the team. After Keith Baxter's bizarre press conference, seeing Fred's familiar face on the sidelines was like a breath of fresh air. The players shared relieved glances and even a few grins, each of them savouring the return of their true leader.

Within days, training sessions were infused with fresh energy. Fred's voice boomed encouragement across the field, his smile now a permanent fixture as he urged the players on. Graham mirrored the mood, nodding approval and offering enthusiastic thumbs-ups from close by. The change was evident on the training pitch. After every goal, the players' wild cheers and pile-on celebrations revealed a team finally letting the shackles off.

Out of nowhere, FC Farce went on an amazing run.

First up was an away game against Worton United, the team they'd stirred up controversy against earlier in the season with Will's imposter twin Gary. Worton's fans hadn't forgotten, holding up taunting signs and launching into chants, mockingly asking, 'Is it really you, Will?'

But Will didn't rise to the bait. He silenced them with a stunning performance, scoring two goals and setting up a third. With each strike, he flashed the crowd a sly grin, blowing them a cheeky kiss after his second. At full-time, he turned around, tapping the name on the back of his shirt with a grin that screamed, 'Do you know who I am now?'

Then came Reefton United at home — a team that had trounced FC Farce 4-1 earlier in the season. Reefton were top four contenders and looked set to win comfortably, but FC Farce's defence held firm under relentless pressure. Each blocked shot and cleared ball earned deafening cheers from the home crowd. As the minutes ticked down, a newfound confidence surged through the team, pushing them on as the scoreline remained goalless.

Sensing an opportunity, Fred urged his team forward in injury time, adopting a dangerous gung-ho approach in search of the winner. Incredibly, it paid off big time. In the final seconds, Nelly Patterson darted past the opposing defender, racing down the wing as fans screamed encouragement. He sent a low, powerful cross into the box, where chaos ensued. The ball ricocheted wildly, deflecting off a Reefton defender's backside before sailing past the stunned keeper.

The stadium erupted, with Nelly racing to the corner flag, arms outstretched as his teammates tackled him in celebration. Meanwhile, the unfortunate centre back nursed the pain of defeat and a sore bottom.

The wins kept coming, with all the luck suddenly going FC Farce's way. Their third match of the month was away to Levelston United, and fortune struck early. Within the first minute, Freddie Thompson fired a sharp pass out to Matty Reynolds on the left, who raced forward towards goal. Levelston's right back lunged, arriving a split second too late and crashing into Matty's standing leg.

The ref had no hesitation in brandishing the red card, leaving the home fans baying for blood and FC Farce's supporters ecstatically leaping to their feet. The man advantage ensured the team grew in confidence, and they eased to a comfortable 2-0 victory.

At full-time, former ballet dancer Tim Jenkins took centre stage, leading victory dances as his delirious teammates cheered along. On the touchline, Fred and his coaching team pulled each other into tight hugs, sharing disbelief and elation. Meanwhile, Graham simply shook his head with a grin.

Just three weeks ago, they'd been nine points adrift. Now they sat third from bottom, just three points behind their nearest rivals with three games to go. If FC Farce could climb above old foes

Vickington Town and stay up, the team would pull off one of the most unlikely turnarounds in football history.

With everything looking rosy, the only negative was a sudden change of attitude in left midfielder Matty Reynolds. Since the wins began piling up, the player had become more of a 'whinger' than a 'winger'. He'd become argumentative, frustrated, and barely seemed to celebrate. Fred had been swept up in the winning streak and barely noticed Matty's sulking. But during their first training session after the Levelston United game, his attitude became impossible to ignore. Fred pulled him to one side.

'Matty, what's the matter with you?' Fred asked wearily. 'We're three wins on the trot, and you're acting like a right miserable bugger. What's going on?'

Matty gave a half-hearted shrug, eyes fixed on the ground. 'I'm fine, boss,' he mumbled.

Fred forced a brighter tone. 'You played well Saturday. That tackle you took for the sending off won us the game. You didn't pick up an injury, did you?'

'Nope.'

Fred sighed. He would've been better off speaking to a brick wall. 'So everything's fine?'

'Yep.' With that, Matty jogged off without so much as a glance back.

Fred watched him run off, unable to shake his growing concern. Matty had never been any trouble before. Had he missed something? Now, with a genuine chance of survival, Fred couldn't afford any cracks in the team's momentum. Although Matty's attitude had soured, he was still giving solid performances, so Fred decided to leave it alone for now. Maybe the lad would snap out of it.

But as the week wore on, Matty's mood only worsened. What he didn't share with Fred was the thoughts that were plaguing his mind — thoughts ironically similar to Fred's own doubts just a few weeks earlier.

In Matty's eyes, he'd done the club a favour in joining them last summer, a huge leap of faith after all the old players had left. Now he'd heard talk of a bigger transfer budget, and in his mind, it was obvious that Fred intended to overhaul the squad. Why should he pretend to be happy about losing his place, or being dumped on the transfer list?

Although Matty had continued to give his all on the pitch, he'd started resenting his manager. Eventually, his frustration grew into a strange belief that relegation might actually be a good thing. That way, the club wouldn't be able to attract the sort of players they would in the Combinations Premier League, and Matty would keep his place in the team. It was a bizarre way of looking at things, but that's where his head was at.

While Matty spiralled into his own conspiracy theories, the rest of the club buzzed with optimism. Tickets for Saturday's crucial home match against Ruffleton Town sold out in minutes. Graham had learnt from the ticketing fiasco before the cup game against Haverstone United, giving the creaking system a much-needed upgrade. On the day of ticket release, Graham held his breath, but there were no system crashes or angry fans.

For a change, it seemed nothing could go wrong at FC Farce! The chairman only hoped that would continue going into their final three games of the season.

⚽⚽⚽

Saturday arrived with beautiful April sunshine and a slight breeze — perfect conditions for football. Fred, who had pretty much resigned himself to relegation just weeks earlier, suddenly felt a rush of nerves now that survival was within reach.

He'd agonised over tactics all week. FC Farce had thrived by adopting an aggressive all-out attacking style, but luck had played a big part. Deciding it would be naïve to keep playing the same way, Fred opted for a more cautious approach, instructing the team to keep it tight and wait for their chance.

Ruffleton Town were no pushovers, sitting eighth with an outside chance of the playoffs. Right from the ref's whistle, they set the tone, moving the ball confidently as FC Farce struggled to get a foothold. The home crowd, a cauldron of noise when the players first took to the field, quietened as Ruffleton took control. Fans shifted restlessly, frustrated by the team's abandonment of the attacking style that had served them so well. But Fred stayed firm, gritting his teeth as he watched Ruffleton press forward, hoping his patience would pay off.

The first half was pretty uneventful, and as the match wore on, Ruffleton Town began to run out of ideas. There had been a few scary moments, not least when their gigantic striker charged into Smithy and managed to knock him clean to the ground, such was his bulk. Fred held his breath, glancing nervously at Shorty on the bench. How on earth would he cope with that lummox up front? Luckily, Smithy was soon back on his feet and signalled that he was OK to continue.

With 20 minutes to go, Fred told his players to go for it. The team poured forward in search of the opening goal, the crowd's energy cranking up a notch. The shift of approach caught Ruffleton Town off guard, with Will Watkins twice slipping his marker and nearly grabbing the opener. With time running out, it looked like FC Farce would have to settle for a point, being left to rue their earlier caution.

Then, on 85 minutes, the pressure finally told. Ex-ballet dancer Tim Jenkins danced around Ruffleton's enormous striker and launched a long ball forward. Barry McGraw outjumped his man to flick it towards Percy Plumb. Percy paused for a split second, then spun and lashed the ball into the roof of the net. 1-0.

The stadium erupted in pandemonium. Even Smithy, after a short pause to catch his breath, raced down to join his teammates in the wild celebrations. The only one not caught up in the frenzy was Matty Reynolds, who hung back with a muted expression.

Fred's bellowing instructions rose above the cheers, urging his players to keep their heads. As the clock reached 90 minutes, coach Steve informed him that Vickington Town's match had ended 1-1. If FC Farce held on, they'd just be a single point behind their rivals with two games to go. The atmosphere tightened as the final minutes ticked by painfully slowly, the entire ground holding its breath.

In the final minute of injury time, the ball found Matty Reynolds on the left. 'Hold onto it, Matty!' Fred screamed hysterically.

But Matty lost concentration. A Ruffleton Town midfielder snatched possession, glancing forward before launching a high, hopeful ball into FC Farce's penalty area. It was the kind of cross that should've been cleared easily, but panic ensued through the defence as Ruffleton's giant striker charged in, sending his marker Clive Harrison flying. The sudden chaos left the net wide open, and the huge forward duly slammed the ball into the net.

'Foul!' screamed the home fans and players in unison, looking expectantly towards the ref.

It was an obvious foul — Ruffleton's towering forward had literally barged Clive off his feet. But to everyone's astonishment, the ref allowed the goal to stand before immediately blowing for full-time. It was an unbelievable decision.

Ruffleton's players wheeled away in celebration, while Fred, barely restrained by his coaching staff, raged at the fourth official. Even Graham completely lost his cool, slamming his wooden seat and earning a splinter for his troubles. The fans who'd been in dreamland just moments earlier sat stunned, the match stolen from their grasp in a single, devastating call.

Later, as Fred moved to console his crestfallen players, he caught sight of Matty's expressionless face, virtually unmoved by the loss.

The draw left FC Farce three points adrift of Vickington Town with only two games remaining. With a daunting away match against Zacton Rovers looming, their survival hopes had taken a huge blow. Realistically, it was out of FC Farce's hands. One more win for Vickington, who held a vastly superior goal difference, would all but guarantee their safety. To take it to the final game, FC Farce would have to better Vickington's result in the penultimate match.

Fred was crushed that the team's efforts hadn't been rewarded.

But he was immensely proud of his players. His team had fought tooth and nail, and grabbing three wins and one draw from their last four games was no mean feat. If it hadn't been for the ref's incompetence, they'd be sitting one point behind Vickington Town, with a much stronger chance of survival.

But Fred couldn't shake the feeling that something was off with Matty Reynolds. Overall, the midfielder had played well enough on Saturday, but his lack of passion was glaringly obvious. Almost unforgivably, after losing possession in the lead-up to Ruffleton's equaliser, Matty hadn't so much as grimaced or looked back. Fred didn't blame Matty for the goal itself, but the lack of remorse and accountability enraged him.

In training the following week, Fred put his frustrations to one side and continued to encourage Matty Reynolds, only to be met with a sulky resistance. Eventually, his patience wore thin.

Pulling Matty aside, Fred looked his player up and down. 'What's with you? This attitude has to stop.'

Matty stared back, his expression blank. 'Nothing's wrong.'

Fred's voice tightened. 'Then why do you look like you couldn't give a shit whether we win or lose?'

For a brief moment, Matty was tempted to blurt out what was bothering him. But he quickly brushed the thought aside, deciding there was little point.

Instead, he gave his all-too-familiar shrug. 'Think what you like,' he muttered. 'I'll do my talking on the pitch.'

Fred scoffed as Matty turned to walk away. 'Funny that, you really did your talking when you fell on your arse and gave the ball away for their goal!'

His sarcasm was lost on Matty, who kept walking, but the encounter left Fred fuming. He was sorely tempted to bench Matty for the crucial game against Zacton Rovers. But with a lack of options on the bench, he reluctantly decided to stick with him. Meanwhile, Matty himself wondered if he wanted to be involved at all, but carried on for the sake of his teammates.

Saturday finally came, and the team made their way to Zacton. The situation was clear. To keep their survival hopes alive until the final day, FC Farce had to better Vickington Town's result. Although Fred would've jumped at this scenario a few weeks ago, he couldn't help but beat himself up over the missed opportunity against Ruffleton.

Backed by a bumper away following, Fred paced the touchline anxiously, watching his 11 starting players as they warmed up. Well, 10 actually, as Matty was nowhere to be seen. Scanning the pitch, Fred's anger simmered as he spotted Matty over by the Zacton Rovers players, laughing and joking with Dan Barton, Zacton's towering centre back and an old mate of his.

'Matty!' Fred bellowed. 'Get back over here!'

Matty rolled his eyes and jogged over, as if it was some kind of inconvenience to warm up with his teammates. Fred ground his teeth but let the matter slide. He had more important things to worry about.

Fred grappled with tactics. The cautious approach against Ruffleton had stifled their play until he'd finally told them to push forward. If they'd attacked from the start, they might have been out of reach before the last-minute equaliser. So this time, he instructed his players to go all out with the aggressive style that had spurred their recent revival. It was a brave or reckless approach — only time would tell.

By half-time, the gamble had gone horribly wrong. FC Farce trailed 2-0, and if it hadn't been for Smithy's heroics, Zacton Rovers would've already been out of sight. As the players trudged off the pitch, word came through that Vickington Town were leading 1-0. In the away section, the fans sat deadly silent — even the die-hards knew it looked hopeless. As it stood, FC Farce trailed Vickington by six points.

Fred felt the weight of his own tactical instructions bearing down on him. Their kamikaze style had backfired horribly. But the team needed goals, so there was no point in changing approach.

Facing his downbeat players, Fred attempted to take the sting out of the situation.

'Look, you don't need me to tell you we're probably going down,' he admitted, forcing a half-smile. 'Just go out and try and enjoy it. Whatever happens, I'm proud of each one of you.'

With the pressure lifted, the team took the pitch with renewed vigour. Just two minutes into the second half, Clive booted a hopeful ball downfield, where Barry McGraw wrestled free of his marker and laid it off to Percy Plumb. Percy quickly found Will Watkins in space, who coolly slotted it into the bottom corner. 2-1. Suddenly the noise levels in the away end went up a notch, more in hope than expectation. Graham's fists punched the air as he dared to dream of an impossible turnaround.

As the game restarted, Fred considered making some changes to keep up the momentum. The obvious choice was Matty, who'd been largely ineffective and looked indifferent all game. Fred gave him one last chance, storming the touchline to berate and shout at him, hoping the intensity would shock him into some kind of response.

Fred's attempt to motivate Matty fell flat. Ignoring his manager's ranting and raving, Matty clenched his jaw, muttering, 'Why should I bust a gut when he's just going to get rid of me?' Instead of proving his worth, he spent the next few minutes deliberately running out of position, barely bothering to track back. Fred's patience finally snapped, and he signalled for his substitute to start warming up.

What happened next was astonishing. Feeling unfairly targeted by his manager, Matty decided he'd had enough. As play continued, he suddenly dropped to the ground, arms crossed defiantly, and sat down in the middle of the pitch. His teammates stared in disbelief.

'Matty, what are you doing?' they cried. But he remained rooted to the spot, their words falling on deaf ears. Supporters from both teams looked on in amazement.

On the sidelines, Fred stood frozen, trying to process what he was seeing. This wasn't an injury — Matty was literally sitting on the grass in protest. Once the shock wore off, Fred exploded.

'Matty!' he bellowed. 'What the bloody hell are you doing? Get up right now!'

But Matty just completely ignored him. A ripple of confusion spread around the stadium, and even the ref seemed unsure whether to stop play. With no injury to address, he shrugged and signalled for the game to continue. Meanwhile, the FC Farce bench frantically gestured towards the ref to make a sub.

Then things took another bizarre turn. Dan Barton, Zacton's centre back who'd had a chinwag with Matty before the game, decided to join his pal's protest. Trotting over, he plopped down next to Matty, arms folded in solidarity.

'I'm with him!' Dan cried dramatically.

The spectacle left the stadium in uproar. Dan's loyalty might have seemed admirable — unless you happened to be a Zacton Rovers fan. Now it was their manager's turn to blow his fuse.

'Dan!' he yelled, hopping up and down on the spot. 'What in God's name are you doing? Get up and play!'

Finally, the ref had seen enough. He blew his whistle and trotted over to the pair, brandishing red cards for both players. The red-faced managers shook their heads in disgust as Matty and Dan trudged off the pitch and headed down the tunnel together, leaving both sides to play with 10 men.

The double sending off inexplicably worked in FC Farce's favour. Zacton lost a crucial defender, while FC Farce lost a stroppy winger who'd been more of a hindrance than a help. Under Fred's instructions, the away team piled forward in search of an equaliser. Zacton's defence held firm for as long as they could, but in the 80th minute, Gavin O'Donnell slipped the ball through to Will Watkins, who picked out an unmarked Percy Plumb. The hesitant striker took his time to size up the shot, before calmly slotting it past the flailing keeper. 2-2.

As players and fans celebrated, news came through that Vickington Town had just conceded an equaliser. In an incredible turnaround from half-time, FC Farce now needed just one goal to take their survival hopes to the final day. With Fred, Graham, and the supporters roaring them on, the players surged forward in search of a winner. Zacton continued to defend resolutely, and as three minutes of injury time were signalled, it looked like FC Farce would fall agonisingly short.

Then, in the 92nd minute, FC Farce won a corner. With Fred's nod, Smithy charged forward at a speed that scarcely seemed possible for a man of his size. His presence alone caused mass panic among the Zacton defenders. The corner came swinging in, and Smithy leapt for a dramatic diving header — missing the ball completely. Taking several defenders with him, the ball bobbled loose, landing at the back post for Will Watkins to nod home. The away end erupted in delirium.

The final whistle blew moments later, and all eyes turned to an agonising wait for Vickington Town's result. Still stunned at the turnaround, Fred took a sharp intake of breath. If Vickington scored, the second half comeback would be for nothing.

'Please,' he pleaded, eyes fixed to the floor as if the weight of the whole season rested on his shoulders.

After what felt like an eternity, the news arrived — Vickington's game had ended in a draw. The wild celebrations continued, with Fred and his coaching staff embracing the players in pure elation. From the stands, Graham burst with pride at the jubilant scenes.

Somehow, FC Farce had taken it to the final day.

CHAPTER 12

MAY — FINAL DAY FARCE

FC Farce's improbable victory sent Henlon into mass hysteria. Everywhere you went, people were buzzing about the team's miraculous turnaround. The club had gone from a laughingstock, lurching from one disaster to the next, to the pride of the town. Even non-football fans were swept up in the excitement of the team's stunning revival. FC Farce had captured everyone's hearts.

Amidst the euphoria, Matty Reynolds' remarkable protest was almost forgotten. His red card meant he'd miss the crucial final game — not that Fred would've considered picking him. But ironically, Matty's antics had helped turn the game in FC Farce's favour, summing up the absurdity of their entire season.

Before tearing up his contract, Fred called Matty in to give him one final chance to explain himself. Realising his days were numbered, and having had time to reflect on his crazy on-field protest, Matty finally saw the stupidity of his actions and opened up.

'I'm... I'm sorry, boss,' he stammered, tears rolling down his cheeks. 'Now the club's come into money, I thought you'd want to get rid of me.' He sniffled, wiping his face with his sleeve, before looking up at Fred.

'Please,' he begged, his voice trembling. 'Give me another chance.'

The manager stopped in his tracks, seeing a familiar look of self-doubt in Matty's troubled eyes. Fred had been plagued by the same negative thoughts only weeks ago. He'd foolishly chucked in his own job, and Graham had given him another chance.

After a few moments of deliberation, he put his hand on Matty's shoulder. 'Alright,' he said, softening. 'You're still part of my plans.'

Matty's relief was evident. After apologising publicly to the fans, he promised to repay the manager's faith. With that, Fred agreed to draw a line under the incident, and another crazy chapter in FC Farce's season was put to bed. Attention turned back to the small matter of Saturday's do-or-die match.

⚽⚽⚽

The win against Zacton Rovers left FC Farce just one point behind Vickington Town. But with a goal difference of -21 to Vickington's -3, a draw wouldn't be enough — even if Vickington lost.

To stay up, FC Farce had to beat Hexton United and hope Vickington Town failed to win at Reefton United. Only a few weeks ago, relegation had seemed inevitable. But now, after their incredible run of form, the thought of falling short would be devastating.

Demand for tickets was unlike anything they'd ever seen. To Graham's relief, the upgraded ticket system coped for the second time without any drama, but thousands of fans were still disappointed. After glancing at the website's traffic report, Graham reckoned they could've filled the stadium five times over.

Excitement and tension built throughout the week, and Graham was determined to keep a lid on things. The Wednesday before the match, he treated his entire coaching team and players to an end-of-season meal. It was his way of thanking everyone for their efforts and making sure they stayed relaxed before the weekend's crucial encounter.

He booked a table at his favourite Italian restaurant. Suffice to say, alcohol was off the menu, not that the players needed reminding. As they arrived, the waiter greeted them warmly.

'Good evening, gentlemen,' he said politely. 'Your table isn't quite ready yet. Would you like to order some drinks while you wait?'

Graham smiled. 'No problem,' he said, ordering a round of soft drinks for the group.

But before the drinks even arrived, the waiter reappeared, looking visibly concerned.

'Um, I'm afraid there's been a mix-up,' he said, wearily. 'We've double-booked your table and the restaurant is fully booked. I'm terribly sorry, but we won't be able to accommodate you tonight.'

Graham felt a flash of irritation, but kept his cool. He wasn't about to make a scene and ruin the evening.

'That's a shame,' he replied calmly. 'But mistakes happen. We'll find somewhere else.' He quickly cancelled the drinks order, and the 30-strong group headed out to consider their next move.

Just as they settled on an alternative venue, an agitated group of staff from the Italian restaurant approached, led by the waiter who'd given them the news about the double booking. Graham smiled, perhaps they'd managed to find a table after all?

Instead, the lead waiter pointed his finger accusingly at Graham, launching into a furious tirade.

'Oi! You stole from our restaurant!' he shouted hysterically. 'You need to pay us right now!'

Graham was open-mouthed. 'What on earth are you talking about?' he demanded. 'We didn't even have anything. You just told us you double-booked our table!'

'You stole 27 cokes from us!' the waiter shrieked.

'Are you insane?' Graham cried. 'We ordered those before you said there was no table. You agreed to cancel our drinks order!'

The waiter flatly refused that was the case, shaking his head emphatically. With the back-and-forth escalating, a flashing police car hurtled towards the scene. As the policeman approached, eyeing the group suspiciously, it became clear his sudden appearance was no accident.

'Here they are!' the waiter wailed, pointing wildly. 'Here are the thieves!'

The policeman folded his arms. 'What have you got to say for yourselves, gentlemen?'

Graham sensed the situation beginning to spiral out of control. They were clearly being set up by the restaurant, but he was fully aware of how it could be misinterpreted in the local press. He glanced at his worried players and sighed, deciding to defuse the situation for the sake of Saturday's game.

'Look, officer,' Graham explained calmly. 'There's been a misunderstanding. We were supposed to be dining at the Italian restaurant, but they double-booked the table and said they couldn't serve us. I asked to cancel our drinks order, and then we left. I apologise if there's been any miscommunication, and I'm happy to pay for the cokes that we unfortunately didn't get to drink.'

The policeman raised an eyebrow and turned to the lead waiter. 'You called the police over unpaid Coca-Colas?'

The waiter suddenly grew flustered. 'Well, yes... I, uh...'

'Enough,' the officer interrupted. 'There's clearly been a misunderstanding. Mr Stavros, I suggest you apologise to Mr Farce and his group for wrongly accusing them of stealing, and let us go back to catching the real criminals.'

The waiter looked at the floor. 'Sorry,' he mumbled.

'Apology accepted,' Graham replied brightly.

The policeman nodded. 'Excellent, now let's all get on with our evenings. Oh, and Graham, good luck to the team on Saturday.' With that, the waiters shuffled back to the restaurant, and the policeman drove away.

Graham shook his head and turned to Fred. 'Can you believe that?'

'I know,' Fred chuckled. 'That's what happens when you stick to soft drinks!'

The chairman laughed. 'C'mon, lads,' he called to the group. 'That's enough excitement for one evening. Takeaway pizzas at my place it is!'

Graham couldn't help but think that escaping arrest just days before the game had to be a good omen. Maybe it was a sign they would pull off an even greater escape on Saturday...

⚽⚽⚽

As usual, Fred's alarm blared on Saturday morning with a piercing shriek, but he'd already been awake for hours. He'd hardly slept a wink in anticipation of the clash against Hexton United. He was quietly confident that Vickington Town would slip up, but had no idea whether his own lads could do the business. Despite his recent antics, the suspended Matty Reynolds would be a big miss. The manager's only option was to start inexperienced 17-year-old Zach Poulter on the left.

The other thing that had kept him up was how to approach the game. In recent matches, they'd swung between going gung-ho and remaining cautious, each bringing mixed results. So the manager decided to meet in the middle — instructing his team to keep it tight in the first half and go all out in the second. He just prayed Vickington wouldn't already be out of sight and render the result meaningless.

Meanwhile, Graham felt strangely relaxed about the occasion. After everything FC Farce had been through, he had come to believe they could survive anything. This final day, of all days, also marked the first anniversary of his father's death. Graham knew his dad would be watching, kicking every ball and roaring with pride. With the old chairman in their corner, he was convinced that fate would decide the outcome.

As they arrived at the ground, the atmosphere was electric, several notches above anything they'd seen all season. Hours before kick-off, cheering fans in dark green shirts crowded the streets, rallying behind the team and showing their appreciation for the team's amazing end-of-season comeback. When the players took to the pitch to warm up, they were met with a deafening roar. Today, the supporters were ready to give everything for their team.

With the atmosphere red-hot, the nerves really jangled. In the dressing room, Fred had one final rallying cry for his players.

'Lads,' Fred began. 'The run you've been on over the past month has been incredible. Whatever happens today, you're all winners in my eyes...'

The lads remained deadly silent, hanging on their manager's

every word.

'But bollocks to that!' Fred cried, a fierce grin breaking through. 'Let's destroy this lot today and finish the job. C'mon, FC Farce!'

'C'mon, FC Farce!' they roared back.

Fully psyched up, the lads piled into the tunnel, stepping out onto the pitch to a sea of dark green flags and a thunderous wall of noise. Fred took a deep breath as he entered the dugout. This was it — there was nothing more he could do now. Meanwhile, Graham looked to the heavens, feeling his father's presence. Amidst the deafening atmosphere, the shrill sound of the referee's whistle signalled the start of the match.

From the first minute, FC Farce immediately found themselves under the cosh. Any hopes that their mid-table opponents might take it easy were soon quashed, as Hexton United quickly went on the front foot. Hexton played like a team without fear, while FC Farce struggled to cope with the enormity of the situation. In the first 10 minutes, Smithy was forced into two smart saves to keep the game goalless.

Fred paced the touchline, barking instructions, but the form that had carried them through this far seemed to desert them. At the back, the centre back pairing of Clive Harrison and Tim Jenkins looked particularly unsettled, made worse by partially deaf Clive struggling to hear his teammate over the deafening crowd noise.

Meanwhile, Matty Reynolds' left midfield replacement Zach Poulter struggled to get into the game. Making his full league debut, he spent much of the half chasing shadows. Left back Barry McGraw tried in vain to cover his inexperienced teammate, but the whole side looked increasingly unbalanced.

Suddenly, midway through the first half, FC Farce were gifted a golden opportunity. As Hexton United surged on the attack, right back Ollie Wright made a perfect tackle, immediately punting the ball forwards. With Hexton's defence exposed, Gavin O'Donnell threaded the ball through to Percy Plumb, leaving him one-on-one with the keeper. The crowd screamed in anticipation of seeing the opening goal.

Percy hesitated, ignoring cries of 'Shoot!' that bellowed from the stands. His delay allowed a defender to swoop in and steal the ball with a last-ditch tackle. Mass groans of frustration echoed throughout the ground, while Fred kicked the turf in anger. How many more chances like that would they get?

As the half wore on, Hexton United tried to take advantage of FC Farce's frailties at the back. A misplaced pass from Freddie Thompson sent the opposition charging forward, only for Clive Harrison's last-ditch tackle preventing a disaster. FC Farce were under constant bombardment, and it was a huge relief when the fourth official signalled two minutes of injury time.

'Keep going lads!' Fred shouted, catching sight of the fourth official's board. 'Just get to half-time level.'

But incredibly, FC Farce went one better. In a carbon copy of Percy's Plumb's missed opportunity, the ball was cleared from defence and picked up by Gavin O'Donnell. His hopeful ball forward landed at the feet of Will Watkins. Will smashed the ball towards the goal first time, catching the keeper off guard. It soared past the outstretched gloves and into the back of the net.

The roof practically came off as players piled onto Will in celebration. 1-0 to FC Farce. With Vickington Town's game still goalless, as it stood, FC Farce were safe.

Immediately after the game restarted, the ref blew for half-time. The half couldn't have gone any better. As the team trotted off to a thunderous reception, Graham wore a grin as wide as the goalmouth, feeling his pre-match optimism come to fruition. The job was only half done, but the ecstatic fans began to believe that this could truly be their day.

In the dressing room, Fred tried to bring his celebrating players back down to earth. He was thrilled with the scoreline, but knew they were fortunate to be in front. Taking the lead had created a fresh dilemma. Last week, they'd had nothing to lose at half-time — going all-out attack in the second half was a no-brainer. Now it was going their way, the manager didn't know what to do next!

Gathering his thoughts, he finally addressed his team. 'Nothing silly, lads,' Fred urged. 'Keep things tight and look for chances on the break. Let's just have a nice, non-eventful 45 minutes for once!'

As the lads headed back out to a hero's welcome, the manager shook his head. 'As if anything at this club was ever that simple,' he muttered.

The atmosphere was white-hot as the match kicked off for the final 45 minutes of the season. Having survived the first half onslaught, the fans urged the team to finish the job quickly, with one eye on events at Vickington Town's match. Meanwhile, Fred gestured towards his players to keep their shape.

Roared on by the vociferous crowd, FC Farce came close to extending their lead twice in the opening minutes. Fed through by his strike partner, Will Watkins lashed the ball goalwards, shaving the crossbar. Minutes later, Gavin O'Donnell unleashed a stunning shot from distance, only for the ball to cannon back off the crossbar. As the noise decibels climbed, it seemed a second goal was inevitable.

Then, disaster struck. From a corner, FC Farce committed far too many players forward, leaving gaping holes at the back. Hexton United quickly cleared the ball, leaving a two-on-one against Tim Jenkins. The poor centre back didn't know whether to commit for a tackle or back off and hold his line. Caught in two minds, he stumbled backwards and landed in a crumpled heap on the floor. With Smithy forced off his line, the Hexton striker calmly side-footed to his unmarked teammate, who rolled the ball into the empty net. 1-1.

The crowd was stunned into silence. After such a promising start, conceding so cheaply was a crushing blow. FC Farce were suddenly staring relegation in the face, with just over 30 minutes to save themselves. Graham looked on open-mouthed, jolted to the realisation that fate could only carry them so far. After mourning the painful equaliser, Fred rallied at his shell-shocked players to get their heads up and push forward.

But the goal knocked the stuffing out of FC Farce. From having their tails up, the team suddenly became a bag of nerves, making basic, unforced errors. Their nerves were reciprocated in the stands, where frustration mounted with every misplaced pass. Meanwhile, Hexton played with growing confidence, missing two gilt-edged opportunities to inflict further damage.

Fred felt the game slipping away. After making a couple of substitutions, he instructed his players to raise the tempo and attack. With 15 minutes left, it was now or never. Nelly Patterson, a passenger for most of the half, picked the ball up and made a trademark run down the wing, flying past his man and sending a cross just millimetres beyond Will Watkins' outstretched leg. Encouraged by the renewed energy, the passionate crowd roared the players on, raising the noise levels once again.

Hexton United were still very much in the game, and for a few tense minutes, it looked like either side could grab the lead. Suddenly, another chance fell FC Farce's way. Despite a shaky start, Matty Reynolds' replacement Zach Poulter had quietly grown into the game. Standing close to goal, Zach shimmied past his marker and looked up to find one of his teammates.

Seeing no options, the player confidently turned and struck with his left foot. The keeper thought he had it covered, but couldn't reach it — the ball ricocheting off the underside of the crossbar and dropping into the net. It was a goal-of-the-season contender. FC Farce had regained their lead with just five minutes left.

'Yesssss!' The scenes were sheer pandemonium, and it took several minutes to restore order. Grown adults hugged each other, some openly wept, and a few even spilled onto the pitch before being shepherded back by the referee and players.

'Come back on when we win!' Clive Harrison shouted, grinning as the delirious crowd eventually returned to the stands.

As Fred picked himself up from the floor, still catching his breath from the wild celebrations, he noticed Matty Reynolds cheering louder than anyone, clapping his replacement's goal as if he'd scored himself. Fred smiled heartily — in that moment the player redeemed himself. Meanwhile, Graham glanced upwards, silently thanking his father for the intervention.

Sprinting to join his teammates, Smithy unfortunately tweaked his hamstring during the raucous scenes. Unable to continue, Fred was forced to replace him with Shorty, making just his second appearance of the season. Glancing towards the less-than-imposing keeper, Fred prayed for the ball to stay as far away from his goal as possible. But FC Farce defended manfully, preventing Smithy's replacement from being tested.

As the end of normal time approached, with the tension unbearable, all eyes were on the fourth official. When he finally held up his board, there were gasps of disbelief throughout the stands. *Seven* minutes added time! With supporters bracing themselves for a further period of agony, the atmosphere was stifled until a deafening cheer suddenly went up around the whole ground.

'Vickington Town's game has finished 1-1!' FC Farce supporters cried to one another, scarcely able to believe it was really happening. Now, if the team held on, they were definitely safe. With sweat pouring down his face, Fred continued to bark instructions.

Despite the incredible pressure, FC Farce held on to possession confidently as the final seconds ticked by. Chants of 'We are staying up!' boomed around the ground, with fans edging towards the sidelines for the inevitable pitch invasion. As the team battled through the final few moments, the crowd hysterically mimicked the ref's whistle, desperate for him to blow for full-time.

With less than 15 seconds left, Hexton United went forward for a rare, final attack. Their right midfielder picked the ball up, and with no supporting teammates, began a hopeful run towards FC Farce's goal. As he entered the edge of the box, skipper Clive Harrison made a strong but fair tackle, booting the ball away from danger. The crowd erupted in premature celebration. Surely that was it?

Then came a devastating twist, shattering the jubilation.
PENALTY!

The referee's whistle pierced the air, and horror swept through the ground. It was a monumental call. Hexton United had barely appealed, yet the ref pointed to the spot, judging Clive's clean tackle as a foul.

Outraged FC Farce players swarmed the referee, while Fred and his coaching staff screamed at the fourth official to intervene. Fans clutched their heads in agony, some too shocked to react. Others attempted to storm the pitch in fury, only to be forcibly held back by frantic stewards. Meanwhile, Graham stood motionless, staring at the floor in complete turmoil, as the stadium's mood swung from euphoric joy to overwhelming despair.

FC Farce's fate now rested on the shoulders of Shorty — who hadn't even touched the ball yet.

The penalty would be the last kick of the game. As Hexton United's forward confidently picked the ball up, even the most optimistic FC Farce fan would've had little hope. Shorty's lack of height was almost comical. Even a tamely hit shot in the corner would easily beat him. But still, Shorty took a deep breath and tried to make himself look as imposing as possible.

On the sidelines, Fred braced himself for the worst. 'C'mon Shorty,' he urged, through gritted teeth.

With the ball on the spot, the crowd fell deadly silent, every eye fixed on Hexton United's striker. The referee blew his whistle, and the striker's run-up oozed confidence, his strides purposeful and determined. He struck the ball with power, sending it hurtling goalwards. For a split second, it looked destined to hit the back of the net.

But then, an unbelievable twist. In the blink of an eye, Shorty leapt like his life depended on it, fingers outstretched, and somehow managed to tip the ball onto the post. The defence charged towards the ball and booted it away from danger. FC Farce's pint-sized substitute keeper had just pulled off a miraculous save to keep them up.

The incredible moment sparked an outpouring of sheer ecstasy. Graham, Fred, the coaching team, and thousands of delirious fans spilled onto the pitch to celebrate FC Farce's extraordinary survival. Flares lit up the air, and a carnival atmosphere engulfed the ground. Players were hoisted onto fans' shoulders, sharing this once-in-a-lifetime moment with their heroes. Shorty, beaming from ear to ear, stood taller than he'd ever dreamed, a legend in the heart of the celebrations.

The scoreboard flashed: 'Full-time — FC Farce stay up!'

On the pitch, Fred and Graham embraced, tears streaming down their faces. They had lived and breathed every possible emotion that season. Just weeks ago, the team had looked doomed. Now, against all odds, they had pulled off a miracle.

Amidst the wild scenes, the referee found himself buried under a heap of delirious fans. After what seemed like an eternity, the red-faced official finally wriggled free, furiously blowing his whistle in a state of panic. He was clearly trying to get a message across to the chaos around him. Fred froze, his heart skipping a beat. *What was he trying to say?*

Spotting Graham and Fred, the referee hurried over to deliver the crushing news.

'Guys, guys,' he panted, struggling to catch his breath. 'I'm really sorry, but your keeper moved off his line. The penalty will have to be retaken. We need to get everyone off the pitch *now*.'

Fred and Graham stared at him, dumbfounded. It was a gut-wrenching turn of events. They'd just been dancing and hugging random strangers in celebration of FC Farce's survival. Now, they were being told it wasn't over.

There was no way the game could restart. Hundreds of fans were still celebrating on the pitch, some even swinging from the goalposts. Stewards tried in vain to clear the pitch, but the sheer number of fans made it impossible.

When one of the swinging supporters finally snapped the crossbar in half, the referee threw his hands up in exasperation and officially abandoned the game. Meanwhile, oblivious fans continued to ecstatically celebrate FC Farce's survival.

Unable to make sense of it all, Graham stared at Fred, his face

drained of colour.
 'So… what the hell happens now?'
 Their season had officially descended into a farce.

CHAPTER 13

THE AFTERMATH

The chaotic conclusion to FC Farce's final match had the whole football world talking. The team were used to making the headlines that season, but the penalty aftermath was on another level. The so-called 'season decider' had ironically left more questions than answers, and the league officials needed to find a quick resolution. If they weren't already fed up with FC Farce, they certainly were now.

There were so many implications to consider. With FC Farce and Vickington Town's fates hanging in the balance, the officials faced several conflicting options. Could FC Farce's 1-0 victory over Hexton United stand? Or should it be ruled as a draw or a loss, meaning Vickington Town survive? Or would the match need to be replayed? After the premature celebrations, the pitch was in disarray — could it even be played elsewhere?

Of course, the real winners were the media, who had a field day covering the story. Headlines from 'Final Day Farce' to 'FC Farce F*ck Up' dominated the back pages, with dozens of media outlets scrambling for soundbites from both clubs. Eager reporters stoked old fires by bringing up the bad blood from the infamous December scoreboard incident. With all the bizarre events at FC Farce that season, the media frenzy was almost second nature. But the hysteria was a whole new experience for Vickington Town.

Naturally, both managers were convinced that the decision should go in the favour of their own side. Fred argued that the penalty should never have been awarded in the first place, and that alone was enough for the result to stand — the fact that Shorty had marginally come off his line was irrelevant when the game was all but over. Meanwhile, Vickington Town's manager insisted that the 1-0 scoreline couldn't possibly stand, and since

FC Farce's overzealous fans had caused the abandonment, the result should go against them by default.

The drama captivated fans nationwide, many of whom had never even heard of the lowly Combinations Premier League. A national sports radio station ran a poll: 'Should FC Farce or Vickington Town be relegated?' The results were nearly split 50/50, reflecting just how divisive and complex the league officials' decision had become.

Opinionated football fans pitched in their own solutions, some more practical than others. One chuckling fan suggested dressing the managers up in sumo suits for a wrestling match to settle the outcome. To be fair, after a season of such madness, he wasn't entirely off the mark.

In the end, the league officials had to come up with a sensible solution. For what felt like the hundredth time that season, they called a formal hearing to decide the outcome. Set for the following Thursday, each passing hour ticked by painfully slowly for Graham and Fred, both gripped by the intense emotions that only football can stir. Graham, once a reluctant chairman but now fully committed to the club's cause, understood this better than anyone.

After days of reflection, the men were united in defiance. They'd won that game fair and square. 97 minutes of football shouldn't be undone by 10 seconds of chaos. And even if the penalty had been retaken, who could say it would have definitely gone in? Their nerves were shredded, but they couldn't see how the league could justify overturning the victory.

⚽⚽⚽

The night before the big day, Fred and Graham met at The Brown Bull — the pub where they'd gotten unintentionally drunk before the memorable fans' forum. This time, they held back, sharing just one drink in quiet solidarity rather than propping up the bar.

Slowly sipping his pint, Fred eyed his chairman. 'So, what's the gut feeling?'

'My view hasn't changed since yesterday,' Graham replied. 'I don't see how it *can't* go our way.'

Fred chuckled, raising his glass. 'Even after our track record this season?'

'Well, yes, that's a slight concern,' Graham said with a smirk. 'But if the league rules against us, we won't take it lying down. We've faced worse this season, and we can beat this too.'

'Agreed.' The pair clinked glasses, finished their pints, and went home to endure another sleepless night.

The next morning, Fred and Graham wrestled past the media scrum and anxiously made their way into the hearing. Vickington Town's manager and chairman arrived moments later, joining them in the hearing room. Greeting the opposition, the league official couldn't resist a cheeky dig at FC Farce's expense.

'Gentlemen, thank you for joining us,' he began brightly. 'If either of you happens to get lost on your way out, Fred or Graham will be happy to show you the way. They've practically got season tickets here.'

'Very funny,' Graham muttered, rolling his eyes as the official sniggered at his own joke. 'Shall we get on with it?'

The attempted banter did little to lighten the atmosphere. The future of two football clubs hung in the balance, and you could cut the tension with a knife as both sides gathered to learn their fate. The hearing was packed to the rafters, a sea of reporters joined by players and fans from both sides. It took what felt like an age to get started, only adding to the mounting drama. Finally, the stern-faced official cleared his throat, silencing the room as all eyes turned to him.

'Thank you for coming everyone,' the official began. 'We appreciate your time today. Unfortunately, the unusual circumstances surrounding this case meant we couldn't give you more notice.' His eyes deliberately flashed towards Fred and Graham.

'Firstly,' he continued, his voice becoming more pointed. 'The events during FC Farce's match against Hexton United beggared belief. Only at this football club could a game end in such a ludicrous manner. I can only apologise to everyone associated with Vickington Town for being dragged into this.'

'Well, that was subtle,' Fred muttered under his breath.

Ignoring the jibe, the official pressed on. 'If it were up to me, I'd award the abandoned match to Hexton United — meaning Vickington Town survive. But unfortunately, I have to consider that 97 minutes had already been played — and that, inconveniently, FC Farce were in the lead.'

Fred and Graham exchanged hopeful glances.

The official continued. 'There is also no way of knowing if the penalty, even if retaken, would have been converted. And replaying the match is simply not feasible this late in the season.'

Graham flashed a quick smile at Fred. It looked like things were going their way.

'So, here is my decision...' he paused dramatically. Vickington's manager and chairman frowned, while Graham and Fred looked ready to punch the air.

'The match won't be replayed,' he announced. 'But to settle the result, Hexton United's penalty will have to be retaken.'

A collective gasp filled the room. Vickington's representatives broke into relieved smiles, while Fred and Graham were left wide-eyed, utterly stunned.

'You what?' Graham spluttered, unable to believe his ears.

'You heard me,' the official replied, unfazed. 'Awarding the game to either side simply wouldn't be fair. There's no time to arrange a full replay, but we can squeeze in a penalty kick. Given the circumstances, this is the fairest decision I can make.'

The official went on to explain the surreal details to the bemused audience. The penalty would be retaken the following day, behind closed doors at FC Farce's training ground. Only the managers, the referee, Shorty, and Hexton United's striker would be allowed to attend. Strictly no fans or media. It was an anticlimax so bizarre, it almost didn't seem real.

Fred clenched his fists. 'You accuse *us* of acting in a ludicrous manner, and then hand down *this* so-called verdict?'

FC Farce fans and players shouted in support of their manager, but the official swiftly cut them off.

'Enough. The decision is final. You do have the right to appeal, of course.'

With that, the room was dismissed. Vickington Town's officials were practically giddy with their good fortune — and who could blame them? The odds of Hexton missing a second penalty were virtually non-existent. Dodging the crowd of press outside, Fred finally turned to his chairman.

'So, what now?' he asked, his voice low.

'We'll go along with this penalty,' Graham replied bleakly. 'But mark my words, unless they somehow miss again, we'll fight it.'

Fred nodded, too worn down to argue. Without another word, both men went home to process yet another bizarre twist in FC Farce's season.

Somehow, they'd survived chaos after chaos to bring their survival hopes to the final day, only for it all to be decided by a lonely training ground penalty kick. After a season filled with so many high-profile incidents played out under the public eye, it was bitterly ironic that this decisive moment would take place at such a soulless setting.

The following morning, there was a strange feeling in the air as Fred and Shorty arrived at FC Farce's training ground, joined by Hexton United's manager and striker. No fans, no chants, no tension — just the muffled shuffling of boots and a thin breeze cutting through the training ground's emptiness.

For Hexton, this was nothing more than an inconvenience. They had long since moved on from the season and were only there to comply with the league's ruling. But for FC Farce, this solitary kick would define their season.

Without the roar and pressure of the crowd, the moment felt hollow, stripped of its usual meaning. Even the referee, often the focal point for crowd frustrations, felt out of place without the intense scrutiny of voracious fans breathing down his neck.

Looking slightly bemused, he explained the process to the two players, trying to maintain some sense of normality.

Unlike the raucous scenes that had defined FC Farce's season, there were no invading sheep, angry farmers, lairy mascots, or protesting players to speak of. Just the referee, two managers, and the two players. Meanwhile, Graham paced at home, agonisingly awaiting the result.

With a few empty words, the referee signalled the players into position. The league had scheduled the kick for 11:30am sharp, and the ref was keen to avoid any final controversy. As the final seconds ticked by, Shorty hopped up and down on the spot, doing his utmost to try and look bigger. Fred mouthed 'good luck' with a quick thumbs-up, before bracing himself for the outcome.

Painfully, there was no final twist. Once again, the striker strode forward with calm precision, taking the shot cleanly. Only this time, the ball easily evaded the despairing Shorty, nestling high into the left-hand corner. The referee gave a small nod, jotting down the result in his notebook.

Just like that, it was all over.

FC Farce were down. It was a bitterly disappointing, damp squib of an ending to their incredible season.

Fred stood frozen, watching as Hexton's manager and player slipped out of the training ground, almost apologetically. Shorty remained on the ground, staring at the floor, unable to lift himself. The referee swiftly made his exit, and Fred composed himself before phoning Graham to deliver the news.

Graham was crushed. For a moment, he couldn't bring himself to muster a single word. Then, after a painful silence, his defiance returned.

'Fred, this isn't over,' he vowed. 'We still have the appeal. I'll get something together tonight. Meet me in the office tomorrow morning at 9 o'clock.'

Emotionally exhausted, Fred had hoped he could finally let

go of this season. But if Graham was ready to fight on, he'd do whatever it took to help him.

⚽⚽⚽

The next day, Fred dragged himself to Graham's office. With pre-season just around the corner, he wondered how much longer they could endure this endless battle. He was ready to take some time off, for his family's sake and Graham's too. But with his chairman so determined to fight the decision, Fred knew he had no choice but to press on.

Putting on his game face, he strode in and asked, 'Alright, Graham, what's our plan for this appeal?'

Graham looked up with an unexpected softness in his eyes. 'Fred… I don't think we should appeal. I've thought about it, and I think it's best if we accept the outcome.'

Fred was completely caught off guard. 'But, why?' he stammered.

Graham sighed deeply. 'We've been through hell together this season. The last thing either of us needs is another dragged-out fight. I don't agree with the verdict any more than you do, but I believe in what we've built here. With you at the helm, I know we can take this team straight back up. We've already won the toughest battle.' The chairman fell silent, his eyes locked on Fred's.

For a moment, Fred was speechless. This was exactly what he wanted to hear, yet he found himself struggling to believe it was truly over. But then, he realised it wasn't ending at all — it was simply the beginning of their next chapter.

'What do you think?' Graham eventually asked, breaking the silence.

Fred nodded, his resolve firming. 'It's for the best, Graham. With your support, and the fight this team's got in them, we'll be right back up there next season.' They shook hands firmly, wishing each other a nice few weeks' rest ahead of another season of madness!

As Graham watched Fred leave his office, a smile crept across his face. It hadn't been an easy decision, but he knew it was the right one. Despite the bitter disappointment of relegation and all the outrageous events throughout the season, FC Farce were in a much stronger position than when they'd started.

The fans, having witnessed the team's grit, heart, and determination — were fully behind them now. They'd be back in numbers next season, ready to back the team's fight for promotion.

For the players, many of whom had once been reserves or cast-offs from other clubs, the season had revived their careers. They'd earned their places and proven what they were truly capable of.

Fred, meanwhile, had more than made up for walking out on the club all those years ago. His team had come agonisingly close to survival, but with his chairman's unwavering trust, he was more determined than ever to lead FC Farce back to where they belonged.

As for Oddsworth, the former council leader was left to nurse the bitterness of his public humiliation. Graham's victory had tarnished his entire career, exposing him for who he truly was. After years of bulldozing over easy targets, he was forced to confront the harsh truth — that the spirit of a football club and its local community is virtually unbreakable.

Finally, the chairman.

Graham, who had once been so reluctant to inherit the club, had come full circle. He had grown into his role, honoured his father's legacy, and transformed FC Farce into a team worth fighting for. The season had pushed him to his limits — but he'd come out stronger, wiser, and more resilient. He knew his father would be proud, laughing his socks off at every chaotic twist along the way.

Although they'd fallen short at the final hurdle, FC Farce now had a solid foundation to rebuild from — a chance to realise their full potential.

Later that evening, Graham raised a glass in tribute. 'Here's to you, Dad,' he said with a smile, knowing that this season had marked the true beginning of the club's revival.

THE END

ABOUT THE AUTHOR

Darryl Barkwill lives in Devon with his wife and two young children, who ensure he never gets a moment's rest — perfect preparation for writing his debut book, FC Farce.

A marketing professional and passionate Plymouth Argyle supporter, Darryl has experienced all the ups, downs, and occasional absurdities of following a lower-league football team. His love of football, alongside his knack for storytelling and sharp sense of humour, inspired him to write FC Farce, a playful celebration of the beautiful (and sometimes ridiculous) game.

Printed in Great Britain
by Amazon